THE VANISHING SHADOW

A JUDY BOLTON Mystery

The Vanishing Shadow

BY
Margaret Sutton

Illustrated by Pelagie Doane

APPLEWOOD BOOKS
Bedford, Massachusetts

The Vanishing Shadow
was originally published in 1932.

Reprinted by permission of the estate of Margaret Sutton.
All Rights Reserved.

———————

For a complete list of titles in the Judy Bolton Mysteries,
please visit judybolton.awb.com.

Thank you for purchasing an Applewood Book.
Applewood reprints America's lively classics—books from
the past that are still of interest to modern readers.
For a free copy of our current catalog, write to:

Applewood Books
P.O. Box 365
Bedford, MA 01730
www.awb.com

ISBN 978-1-4290-9021-6

MANUFACTURED IN THE U.S.A.

"HORACE! HOR———"

The Vanishing Shadow.   Frontispiece (Page 16)

A JUDY BOLTON MYSTERY

THE VANISHING SHADOW

BY

MARGARET SUTTON

AUTHOR OF "THE INVISIBLE CHIMES,"
"THE HAUNTED ATTIC," ETC.

ILLUSTRATED BY

PELAGIE DOANE

GROSSET & DUNLAP
PUBLISHERS   NEW YORK

MORE ABOUT THE AUTHOR
By
MARGARET SUTTON HUNTING

My FATHER was a carpenter, and I was born in 1903 in Odin, Pennsylvania. I was given the name Rachel Irene. My parents, Victor and Estella Beebe, were creative people who encouraged my brother, sister and me to learn at home as well as at the one-room school we attended. Papa wrote songs, played the fiddle and the organ, and taught us geography, history, astronomy and the theory of evolution. Mama drew wonderful pictures and told us folk stories. We later moved to Coudersport, where I attended high school.

I left home at age 16 and graduated from Rochester Business Institute with highest honors. After working a year as a stenographer, I became a printer and lived in Detroit, Chicago, and New York. In 1924 I married my favorite chess partner and poet, William Sutton, and began writing stories to please his seven-year-old daughter, Dorothy.

My series began with the story of the Austin flood which I told to my stepdaughter and fictionalized so it wouldn't be so sad. Actually, nearly 100 people lost their lives in 1911 when the big dam broke and flooded the town of Austin, Pennsylvania. My family lived three miles above the dam.

I read the stories aloud to Dorothy, chapter by chapter, and she asked me to write them down. Friends encouraged me to seek a publisher, and in 1932 the first Judy Bolton mysteries were accepted by Grosset & Dunlap. My new publishers thought my name, Rachel, too unsophisticated for an author of series books and suggested that I use the name Margaret Sutton. We lived in Brooklyn, near the New York subway, so it was easy for me to take my finished stories to the editor and meet with her personally. A good editor is a wonderful help, especially when you're first getting started.

In the years that followed, each of our five children provided joy, enthusiasm and inspiration. The books were all based on real events, and many of the characters were based on family members and friends. A rude neighbor or unfriendly sales person might become a jewel thief or a kidnapper in the books!

Through my membership in a guild for authors I met many famous people including my best friend, Helen Diehl Olds, who wrote a series of career books. Many of my fans also became dear friends. One girl who first wrote to me when she was 12 years old and signed herself "FF" for "favorite fan" is now writing her own series of books. Some of the students in my creative writing classes have also become published authors.

I had been married for more than 40 years when my first husband died, and I became a bride again when I married Everett Hunting and acquired four grown stepchildren. After many years living in Berkeley, California, I am alone again and living in my native Pennsylvania. I am a great-great grandmother, and in between visits from my family and fans, I am writing my life story.

To Dorothy

CONTENTS

CONTENTS

THE VANISHING SHADOW

CHAPTER I

TWO MYSTERIES

"Hey, Judy!" called Lanky Edna Jenkins. "Get your nose out of that book and come to the mail box."

Judy Bolton looked up with a start. She had supposed herself to be quite alone. Early in the afternoon, knowing from experience that the day would be another hot one, she had searched out the coolest place to be found, under a beech tree not far from the new road, and settled herself to read and watch the men at work.

"There's a letter for you," Edna persisted. "Come for a walk and get it."

"It's too hot. Anyway Grandfather will bring it." Judy tossed aside the book and settled her back against the tree trunk. The storekeeper's daughter was no friend of her own choosing. The tall beech tree and the friendly sumacs along the edge of Dry Brook were bet-

ter company. She liked to hear the workmen
calling to each other as they busied themselves
with shovels and machinery on the new concrete
road which, when completed, would bring her
grandparents nearer town and all the things
Judy loved.

Part of every summer she and her older
brother, Horace, spent at the Smeed farm with
Mrs. Bolton's parents while her father, the town
physician, went away to the seashore for a much
needed rest.

Days were intolerably long and monotonous
in Dry Brook Hollow and the two or three weeks
seemed like so many months to the vivacious
auburn haired girl from Roulsville. At home
she had never lacked for adventure. Her father's business brought her in contact with all
kinds of people as she often went with him when
he made his calls.

Roulsville was a rapidly growing town. It
was situated in a narrow valley three miles below where Dry Brook joined another and larger
stream. A giant white concrete dam had just
recently been completed to supply power for the
paper mill which was the town's big industry.

Below the dam there were stores and banks,
a small theatre and a park in the midst of which

was a round pavilion. Farther down the valley, opposite the old River Street church, was Dr. Bolton's combined home and office.

Judy was feeling a little homesick now as she sat watching the men working on the road. Only a few weeks ago she had watched with more interest a greater work of construction —the Roulsville dam.

Edna stood watching the workmen too. "They're an ugly looking lot," she commented. "Don't look as if they'd seen a Saturday night since New Years."

"They are dirty," Judy agreed. "But that isn't important when you think of what they are accomplishing. Next to the work my father does I think building things is the most worth while."

"Guess you're right," agreed the store-keeper's daughter, "but these men don't look as if they were finding much joy in their work."

Both girls were watching with interest that changed to alarm as angry voices came distinctly to their ears.

"You're paid to keep your mouth shut," they heard one workman say. He stood with shovel upraised and for a breathless moment Judy felt sure she was about to witness a murder. "Another word about that dam and I'll smash your ugly face in," he shouted.

Judy sprang to her feet. "We can't let them kill each other," she cried. "That sounds like the beginning of a terrible fight."

"And the end of it too." Edna pointed an eloquent finger in the direction of the two workmen. "See that little fellow backing away? He's going to keep his mouth shut. He's another sissy like your brother, Horace. He'd do anything that big guy told him to."

Ignoring the unkind remark about her brother, Judy continued to watch the two workmen. The smaller one was backing toward the bushes at the side of the road very near where they were standing. Edna wanted to hide or run away but Judy, attracted to any kind of excitement as a needle to a magnet, insisted upon staying where they were.

"Maybe we can help that little man," she whispered. There was genuine sympathy in her voice.

The big fellow with the stubbly black beard had him by the throat now and he was gasping, "I promise! I—I p-p-promise."

"All right. All right," the other drawled. "But understand now, this gang wants no dealings with squealers. No talk about that pit either. Get me?"

"I get you. C-can I go?"

The big man dismissed him with a grunt and all at once his eyes lit upon the two girls. He turned suddenly on his broad heel.

"What did you two hear?" he demanded.

"N-nothing," Edna stammered.

"And you?" He turned to Judy and she answered frankly and without fear. "I heard everything you said."

"I didn't hurt that little guy, see?" The man was glaring at her. "And I won't hurt you if you keep quiet. Understand?"

Judy did not understand. Her puzzled gray eyes must have told the surly man that much but, for some reason, he turned and went. Both girls uttered a deep sigh of relief.

"Horace would have been scared to death," Edna declared.

"You weren't so brave yourself," Judy retorted in none too friendly a tone. Edna's everlasting gibing about her brother annoyed her. Everybody knew that Horace had been a sickly child but Judy hoped, with little reason, that he was overcoming his timidity as well as his ill health.

"At least he would have been interested in what those men were saying," she defended. "What can they know about the dam?"

"Maybe they worked on it," Edna replied.

"That's so," Judy's face clouded. "But it takes more brains to build a dam than it does to make a road. That dam is beautiful. It doesn't seem as if these ugly men could have had anything to do with it. What do you suppose they meant about the pit?"

"Search me. Come, let's see what's in the mail box to interest me."

This time Judy agreed whole heartedly and the angry, threatening voices were promptly forgotten as her fingers closed upon a square white envelope. It was addressed to Miss Judy Bolton in bright purple ink in an unfamiliar but decidedly interesting handwriting. Judy stared at the bold purple letters and then tore open the envelope and examined the contents.

For a moment she stood transfixed. Two mysteries in one day and this was Dry Brook Hollow where nothing ever happened!

"It's something wonderful," Judy said, concealing the letter behind her back. "Guess."

"Your rich uncle died and left you a fortune."

"I haven't any uncle, much less a rich one.

"Look! Somebody's sent me ten tickets to a dance and spelling bee and I haven't the ghost of an idea who it was."

"Maybe your boy friend. That handsome one with the shovel."

"Edna, don't. He's terrible. I want to forget their ugly quarrel."

"You and I had better both forget it," she replied significantly as she turned to go.

Judy continued to examine the tickets long after Edna's ungainly form had disappeared around the bend in the road. As she did so, a yellow slip of paper fell out of the envelope. It was marked with a single blue cross.

"That's strange," she murmured, turning the paper over in her hand. "What could it mean? Perhaps at the spelling bee——"

She meant to go on purpose to find out who sent the tickets and just why they had marked the paper with a cross. All her life Judy had pined for a mystery to solve but thus far none had come her way. Now there were two, one a simply delightful problem which going to that party might solve and the other so unpleasant that Judy almost wanted to dismiss it from her thoughts.

CHAPTER II

Judy did not often confide in her grandmother. Though kind and charitable at heart, Mrs. Smeed had a stern exterior which repelled confidences. This time, however, the question seemed all-important and she approached her somewhat timidly as she sat paring potatoes at the sink.

"Let me have a knife, Grandma, and I'll help. I want to talk to you."

"About time you learned to help without being asked," said Mrs. Smeed. "Now when Horace is here I don't have all this work to do alone. He always helps just like a girl."

"Oh, I know I'm not as good as Horace," Judy replied impatiently. "I never could be. But I do try to help in the kitchen and I take care of grandfather's chickens and horses."

"Just the work you like to do."

"Please don't talk like that, Grandma. I'm helping pare potatoes now and nobody asked me to." Judy jabbed the knife point viciously into a worm hole just to express what she dared

8

not say. Well, she must bring up the question
of the tickets some time. Might as well do it
right now.

"I got tickets," she began.

"Tickets to what?" demanded Mrs. Smeed.
"Who'd be sending you tickets?"

"I don't know who sent them. That's what
makes it so—so mysterious and exciting.
They're tickets to a spelling bee and dance in
the Roulsville park pavilion. And—they cost
a—dollar. I've spent all my allowance and I
thought maybe with that money Dad left for
us——"

"That's all gone," her grandmother interrupted. "Horace wanted a new suit and I gave
it to him. His salary's got to be kept for college and he needs to look nice if he's going to
be a successful newspaper reporter. Now what
are you snivelling about?"

The injustice of it had hurt Judy and, all of a
sudden, she had burst into a flood of uncon-
trolled tears. This summer had been a succes-
sion of hot, empty days away from the friends
she had made in high school, away from her
parents and with only Edna Jenkins for company. Now that she did have a chance to go
somewhere and enjoy herself, Horace had to

spoil it all. Besides she was a little unnerved from her encounter with the man with the shovel and felt hopelessly unloved and alone. Holding a half-pared potato in one hand and her knife perilously near her face, she buried her head in her apron and sobbed aloud.

"There, there, Judy," comforted her grandmother. "How did I know you wanted the money?"

"Oh, no," she retorted, her eyes flashing, "I never have any use for new clothes. It's always Horace. It's his silly ideas of right and wrong that influence the whole family."

"He's a conscientious boy, my dear," her grandmother chided.

"Conscientious nothing! It's because he's a weakling himself and hates to see other people enjoying themselves. That money was partly mine and he had no right to take it. Any boy with an ounce of courage would have refused it. And you had no right to give it to him either, Grandmother Smeed!"

Before the startled old lady could make a reply to this unexpected outburst of temper Judy had slammed the kitchen door behind her and was hurrying out to the grove where she could brood over her troubles alone.

Under the beech tree by the white roadway
she could enjoy perfect silence. The workmen
would not be there so late in the day and she
could wait until Horace came in sight. Then
she would give him a piece of her mind. Just
because he had been sickly as a boy he seemed
to think he could dominate the whole family
with his ridiculous whims.

Under the beech tree, however, Judy did not
find the calm she had anticipated. A man was
crouching there as if laying in wait for some
one. He was dressed in good clothes but his
face was the same ugly one that had glared
threateningly at his mate as he stood with upraised shovel. Her temper still hot from her
grandmother's unkind words, Judy turned on
him angrily.

"What are you doing here?" she demanded.
"This is my grandfather's land and he has a
sign down there 'No Trespassing.'"

"Yeah? I saw it." He grinned at her.
"Come now, I ain't going to hurt you. I just
brought you a nice little Christmas present."

"What do you mean?"

A grimy hand dove into his hip pocket and
he exhibited the treasure, a necklace of pearls
in three dainty strands. The clasp that fas-

tened them sparkled with small diamonds.
Judy eyed the trinket suspiciously.

"Oh! So I'll keep quiet?"

"You got the idea."

"Quite an idea," she scoffed derisively.
"But this time you picked on the wrong party.
I don't accept bribes from you or anyone."

"You don't, eh?" He glowered at her.

"Indeed I don't."

"Then you'll keep quiet without a bribe!"

He hurled these words at her and was gone
as suddenly as he had appeared, leaving Judy
dazed and uncertain as to what he had been
talking about.

Apparently she had heard something of great
importance and yet—"You're paid to keep
your mouth shut . . . about the dam . . . and
about the pit." That was all.

Some sinister plot was undoubtedly hinged
on those words and since Judy and Edna were
the only ones who had heard them it was their
duty to see that the plot was foiled. But how?
That was the question and, try as she would,
Judy could not think of an answer. Could there
possibly be some connection between this plot
and the blue cross in her letter?

She had been so excited by what she had

overheard and by her unusual discovery in the mysterious envelope addressed in purple ink that she had forgotten the book she had been reading. Perhaps the bearded workman had seen it and been clever enough to suspect that Judy would return for it. She chided herself for her carelessness as she lifted it from its grassy resting place and brushed a caterpillar from the cover. It was one of her new books too. Realizing that Dry Brook Hollow offered little excitement to his adventure-loving daughter, Dr. Bolton always bought her a new supply of exciting stories to read during the summer.

Judy seated herself beside the tree and turned the pages absently. Her own adventures that day had been as exceptional as any of her book heroine's and she wondered, with an apprehensive shudder, what might happen next. That ugly workman had told her she would keep quiet without a bribe.

"How can he keep me from talking?" she puzzled. "And what harm can come of it if I do talk? What is this secret of theirs? And how can I help defeat their plot? Why is it so important that they offer bribes to keep people silent?"

These and many more perplexing questions crowded into Judy's mind as she sat by the tree alone. It was growing late but she had forgotten her grandmother who was left to prepare supper without her help. The book was open on her lap but she had not read a word.

Suddenly a shadow crossed the page, a quick shadow as if something had hurried past and then darted out of sight before she had a chance to see what it was.

Judy looked in all directions. A strange fear had taken posesssion of her. She tried to shake off her misgivings, reasoning to herself that perhaps it was only a cloud passing across the sky. The sun was low on the horizon and it was only natural that shadows should come with evening.

Then it flickered across the page again, distinctly in the shape of a head. Judy sprang to her feet with a startled cry just in time to see the sumacs along the edge of Dry Brook part and something—she could not see what—disappear among the bushes.

CHAPTER III

IT WAS a reckless thing to do but Judy felt that she must see what had caused that ghostly shadow. As if impelled by some invisible force, she darted after it, through the sumacs and on as far as she could see the moving bushes.

Whenever she paused, the shadow would vanish and when she continued her pursuit of it, the bushes ahead would move, ever so slightly. Once she thought she saw something black, and dived in after it. But the thing, whatever it was had eluded her again.

As Judy paused, uncertain and afraid, silence greeted her. It was a silence so absolute that when, a few minutes later, footsteps sounded on the new cement road, she stood almost paralyzed with fear until she realized that it was only her brother, Horace, who had walked up from the station in Roulsville.

Relief flooded her face and she instantly forgot that she had intended to upbraid him for taking her share of the money. Stumbling in her excitement, she made for the road. Her brother was almost out of sight.

"Horace!" she called. "Horace! Wait a minute."

He had not heard her.

"Horace! Hor——"

The word was cut in two, forcibly, by a hand that was clapped across Judy's mouth with such violence that she staggered backward and caught her breath in a quick, terrified gasp.

In the moment before darkness closed over her she saw Horace's retreating figure and knew that he had not heard. She tried to turn, to see what had happened, but something held her in a vice-like grip, gagged her with a strip of blue checked cloth and in another moment she was enveloped in smothering darkness.

She struck out frantically with her hands until they were bound. Then she kicked with the full force of her body but she was powerless to escape and her fate seemed to be in the hands of the swift creature who was carrying her to —she knew not what.

The bag over her head made it almost impossible for her to breathe. Oh, if she could only open her mouth—just one long breath of air. They couldn't smother her. Things like that

didn't happen—didn't happen in Dry Brook
Hollow.

A measure of relief came when she felt herself being thrown into what she presently realized must be a car. It was moving and the
swift current of air that penetrated the bag
over Judy's head made it easier for her to
breathe. At least she wasn't going to be
smothered, but that was small comfort to the
gagged and bound girl who lay helpless in the
back of an unknown car.

Where were they taking her? Oh, if she ever
freed herself they would pay, and pay dearly,
for the crime they were committing. She would
stop at nothing to defeat their wicked schemes.
If keeping people quiet was important enough
to warrant a kidnaping, the schemes themselves must be of enormous proportions. Even
murder——

Oh, she wished she could hear what they were
saying. She would remember when she was
free——

Hoping against hope, she strained her ears
to catch what she could of their conversation.
One voice was low and gruff. That must be the
bearded workman. But the other had a high-
pitched, rasping quality which left Judy uncer-

tain whether the speaker was a man or a woman. The unnatural voice matched the thin, almost chalk-white hands of the creature who had whisked her away. She had not seen its face. Somehow she could not think of this shadow, this phantom, as a human being, but rather as personified terror.

"You've queered our plans," she could hear its voice, "unless we can get rid of the girl. There's only one place . . ." The voice was lowered.

"Is that where we're headed for?" This was the gruff voice of the workman.

"Yes, and if you don't meddle into my plans we'll leave her there until we get this matter of pay straightened out. But if we want to save our own skins we'll beat it as soon after that as we can pack our baggage. Once they find out about the dam——"

"Shut up, you fool! She may be listening."

"She's heard the whole story from your blatting mouth," the high pitched voice returned angrily. "And by the time she's free to talk again——"

"Free to talk!" the other ejaculated. "If you lock her up there she'll be killed along with the rest of them."

In the back seat Judy felt as if she must scream, as if her lungs would burst with the horrified gasps that were choked back into her throat. She would be killed along with the rest of them. Who were these other people? Judy must escape—she simply must. Not only her own life but the lives of others were hanging by a thread. These brutal creatures seemed to have the power of severing that thread. They were contemplating murder!

"That would be just too bad!"

She heard a derisive chuckle and then the workman with more sympathy in his voice than Judy had believed possible.

"Poor kid! Mebbe we can get her to promise."

"Yeah, after she's been locked up and starved she may come off her high perch and if I know human nature once we worm a promise out of her she'll keep it to the letter. And if she squeals——"

The rest of the sentence was drowned by the noise of the car as it turned off on a rough detour, or a country road. Judy was left to guess which. Her body was thrown violently against the back of the driver's seat as they started down hill at full speed.

"Better stop here. Road's too muddy ahead." It was the workman's voice again.

There was a sound of grinding brakes as the car came to a standstill and its two occupants scrambled out. They stood for a moment talking in muffled voices and then one of them swung open the rear door of the car.

As the long, claw-like fingers of her ghostly captor took hold of her again it made Judy's flesh fairly creep. She felt helpless, weak and sick with fear. She could hear a constant roaring sound even after the car had stopped and could not be sure whether it was water near by or merely a buzzing inside her own throbbing head.

She was carried for quite a distance over wet and soggy ground. Water oozed forth with every step and the muffled sound that came to Judy's ears through the bag suggested all kinds of horrors. She thought of drowning, of being strangled, smothered or thrown, bound and gagged as she was, into the swamp.

The air about her was stifling and Judy wondered how much longer she could keep on breathing. The rag over her mouth cut into her cheeks until her face felt numb and her throat parched. If that roaring sound she heard was water, how she wished that someone would pour it over her face and let her take one long refreshing drink.

"Well, here we are. Gimme the key and I'll open it." The workman's voice broke through the sound of roaring water and as he spoke Judy heard the tread of his feet on wooden boards. The key clicked in the lock of a door through which Judy was hurried and then unceremoniously dropped to the floor.

She lay there for more than an hour, stunned and terrified by the noises that came to her ears. There was water, the constant sound of falling water, but Judy could stand that even if her throat was parched with thirst.

It was the noise of incessant hammering that was unbearable. They had started it almost as soon as the door closed after them and Judy had a sickening feeling that she was being nailed as well as locked inside her prison. If that was the case they would probably carry out their threat and leave her to starve unless she promised. Promised what, she wondered. But Judy had no intention of making any promises that would help the dark scheme afoot.

The hammering finally ceased and Judy thought that she must be nailed in like a chicken being taken to the butcher shop in a crate. Thus it startled her when she heard the door opening and footsteps on the floor very near where she was lying.

"Better make quick work of it," the workman advised as the claw-like hands of her captor fumbled about her body, her neck, her face. Judy's blood ran cold. It was as though a serpent were crawling over her. She struggled desperately and then, all at once, discovered that her hands were free. Frantically she tore at the bag but just as her head was clear of it she heard a key outside turn in the lock of the door with a click of finality.

"Goodnight, girlie," called a high-pitched, mocking voice. "I'll be back again in the morning."

CHAPTER IV

IMPRISONED

THE room in which Judy found herself was as dark as a pit. It might even be a pit for all she knew. Her definition of the word was vague and thus it was all the more puzzling what the workman had meant when he had warned his mate to keep still about the pit.

But there must be some means of escape. If she could only see! She felt in the pocket of her dress hoping to find a match, but instead withdrew the pack of tickets to the spelling bee.

"What use are they now?" she thought despondently. "I'll be in here starving while all the young people in Roulsville are enjoying themselves."

She was pacing up and down the rough floor of the dark room shuffling the tickets nervously. Her eyes smarted and she felt sure that there were red welts across her cheeks where the gingham rag had been bound so tightly.

She knew there was no use crying out as her prison was probably a long way from the main

travelled road and even if she did call that
roaring noise outside would drown the sound.
It was no use trying to force open the door
either. Judy learned that definitely after her
first few minutes of frantic storming at the
closed panels.

The tickets she held in her hands only added
to her despondency and when she had grown
weary of shuffling them she started to replace
them in her pocket when her fingers closed upon
something else—a key. Her heart leaped with
a wild hope as she felt along the door until she
found the empty keyhole.

"It might fit! It might fit!" she kept saying
to herself. "It might fit. It might—not."

The last word fell flat as the key slid nearly
through the enormous keyhole.

"I might have known it," Judy sighed as she
sank into the one chair in the closed and locked
room.

There was a cot in the room too but Judy
had no intentions of going to sleep. She had
touched it once and her fingers shrank from
the moist and unclean cover.

The room was stuffy and Judy could find no
evidence of a window. She felt around the wall
and finally, by standing on tiptoe, managed to

reach a sill. Groping in the darkness, she moved the chair over to where she could stand on it. She fumbled for the window and, to her amazement, thrust her hand right through the frame. Beyond was a blank wall of boards, meaning that there was no hope of escape through the window. Perhaps the hammering had been the work of nailing those boards across the one opening in the room.

As the night wore on slight noises seemed more disturbing. The constant roar of the water outside was interrupted now and then by a cracking sound that sent a shudder down the distracted girl's spine. She remembered hearing a similar sound in her own room once after it had just been re-papered. The paper hangers had neglected to remove the old paper, causing the new paper to crack.

But when Judy felt carefully over the walls she discovered that they were nothing but rough boards and never had been papered. The only paper she could find was part of an envelope that had been stuffed into a crack. This she saved as a possible clue to the identity of her captors.

The sound, then, must have come from outside. Perhaps somebody walking close by.

She heard it again and, hoping desperately that some one would hear, screamed, "Help! Help!" with all her might.

The hollow sound of the echo came back as her only answer.

That night seemed endless as Judy alternated between pacing the floor and huddling in a heap on the chair.

Dozens of times she shuffled the spelling bee tickets just to keep her restless fingers busy or else she tossed the key back and forth from one hand to the other. It was the key to their house in Roulsville. Judy had kept it in case she needed more clothes or any little thing from her own room during the summer while her parents were away.

What would they think if they knew what their daughter was suffering? She must find some way to escape before they were notified. Her grandmother might think she had stayed all night with some friend in Roulsville and delay notifying her father until morning. Once before Judy had lost her temper and disappeared after a quarrel with Horace. Then she had stayed all night with Dora Scott, an adventurous chum who had later moved to Alaska. Perhaps Grandmother Sneed would think the

same thing had happened again. She would be
calling up friends all night long. Perhaps
Horace and his grandfather would go out
searching. But they would never think of looking for Judy in a lonely swamp.

The location of her prison puzzled her. She
could think of no swamp anywhere near Dry
Brook Hollow. The new road, when completed,
would go through to Farringdon, the city where
Horace worked as a reporter. The kidnapers
might have turned in that direction over a less
familiar route. When morning came Judy
meant to look out through the keyhole and determine exactly what the surrounding country
looked like.

But morning seemed a century away. Often
Judy had expressed a desire to stay up all
night. It would be something different to do,
something to tell an envying circle of friends.
But now if those dreadful threats were carried
out she might never see her home or friends
again.

It had not occured to Judy, during that night
of suspense, that she was acting courageously
in trying to figure things out instead of giving
way to despair. The one thought that prayed
upon her mind more than any other was the

fact that while she was imprisoned she was helpless to defeat the wicked schemes of her abductors.

"I'm supposed to promise something. But what?" she wondered.

A promise was, after all, a small thing to ask in return for one's life. But promises might be dangerous things.

"And I'd rather die," Judy said to herself with determination, "than take any part in their underhanded plot."

Daylight came at last, unobserved by Judy in her dark prison, until a streak of sifted light streamed down through a crack in the roof.

"Oh!" she cried and sprang to her feet. She had been nodding in her cramped position on the chair.

Now she ran to the keyhole, knelt beside it and peered out expectantly. The rough surface of another board met her gaze and she realized, with a sinking sensation, that the door was propped shut and her view cut off. The same was true of the boarded window. There were just a few narrow cracks through which a little light sifted.

All at once Judy heard a noise outside, a noise which might have terrified another girl but which caused Judy's heart to leap with joy. It was a dog! Perhaps this dumb creature could help her escape. She was a lover of all animals, especially dogs and cats. They seemed to sense her friendliness instinctively.

"Nice doggie! Nice doggie!" she crooned, but was surprised that her advances were met with a low growl.

"Good doggie!" she called softly.

The guttural sounds which came from the animal's throat were manifestly ill-natured and threatening.

"I can make him bark at least," she told herself, and kicked violently against the door.

"That may attract someone's attention," she thought hopefully.

She kicked again with all her might, kicked and banged and pounded against the panels. She paused, out of breath, and, just as she had expected, the dog began to bark furiously.

In another minute footsteps were heard approaching.

CHAPTER V

"Help! Help!"

Judy's piercing cry sounded above the roar of water and the dog's savage barking.

"Down, you cur," she heard a man's voice command.

The disheartening realization that it was the bearded workman again left Judy completely crushed.

"What were you yelling about in there?" he wanted to know.

"I—I was frightened," Judy answered tremulously. "It's awful in here alone. It's—it's still dark."

"Yeah, I know it. We didn't plan no picnic for you. Beginning to feel a bit hungry, eh?"

Judy admitted that she was starved. "And so thirsty," she added plaintively. "Please let me out."

She heard the man chuckle. "A bit more of this and you'll be willing to promise. What?"

There was no answer. Judy took her head in her hands and sat motionless on the chair. If that roaring would stop for a minute she might be able to think of a way out.

"A promise. A promise. A promise."

The words kept whirling around and around in her head. Suddenly she realized that she might faint and that would be terrible. Unconscious, she would be completely in the power of her captors. No, she must not faint. She must not. Oh, that feeling of emptiness! That awful thirst! She swallowed hard and was about to rise to her feet again when she heard another voice outside.

"Think she's giving in, eh?"

"Sounded pretty weak to me," the workman replied. "Did you bring the beads?"

"Right here." He must have indicated a pocket, Judy thought but if he had an idea she would accept that necklace he was mightily mistaken.

"How about it?" the high-pitched voice inquired. "Are you ready to keep still?"

"I'm ready to faint," Judy replied truthfully. "I—I'm afraid I wouldn't know what I was promising. Couldn't I have a drink?"

"Not until you promise."

Promise . . . Promise . . . The word was spinning in her head again. Certainly she was as useless as a mummy now. If she promised . . . promised . . . How binding was a promise? Could she—could she keep it to the letter and still—and still——

"Well," the gruff voice outside inquired. "Have you made up your mind?"

"Wait a minute. I'm thinking."

"You've had all night to think in," the shrill voice derided her. "And we should stand and wait——"

"Leave her alone," the other commanded harshly.

A promise . . . A promise . . . that she would keep to the letter and yet word in such a way that it gave her a loophole of escape. Was it right to make such a promise? Was it wise? What would her father do?

That was the surest way to solve her problem—to try and think what Dr. Bolton would do in like circumstances. He would not let these criminals escape, of that Judy was certain. And the only way to defeat their plans was to free herself so that she could act even if she could not talk.

"Oh, Dad," she murmured, almost as if she

were praying. "If you could only be here—to
tell me—what is right."

In her mind she could hear him saying, as
he had often said, "I can trust your head to
work out a good solution, Judy girl."

"Are you still there?" she called in a strained
voice to the figures outside.

"Yeah, we're waiting."

"Then what is it you want me to promise?
You—you say the words. I'll repeat them."

She heard a surprised ejaculation followed
by a whispered conference. Then the voice
of her captor spoke through the door.

"All right then. Here's the terms."

"Am—am I—making this promise—to you?"
she faltered. She had hoped that the workman, who at least seemed human, would form
the words which she must repeat.

"Yes, to me," he returned coldly. "Say
this: I promise, on my honor, not to speak a
word of what I overhead . . ."

"I promise, on my honor, not to speak a word
of what I overheard."

"Either by the road or in the car."

"Either by the road or in the car," Judy repeated, parrot-like, and stood waiting for the
next sentence of her promise. Instead, how-

ever, she heard the key turning in the door of her prison and before she knew what was happening the bearded workman stood beside her.

"Is that all of the promise?" she gasped.

"Ain't it enough? Now where'll we take you to?"

"Home," she breathed. "To my grandmother's home in Dry Brook Hollow."

"Yeh? And what'll you tell her?"

Judy had not thought of that. She stared at the workman's face in blank bewilderment.

"What *will* I tell her?"

"Tell her you stayed with a girl friend—tell her you stayed in a barn—anything. But don't let on I had any hand in it."

"I see. And I must promise that too?"

"Make her promise it," called the shrill voice from outside. "And hold her till she does."

Promise . . . Promise . . .

Judy pushed her hair away from her hot forehead. She must think. She couldn't let herself feel dizzy. The key jingled in her pocket as she sank, almost fainting, into the chair. The workman caught at her skirt and kept her from falling but the jingle of the key had given her an idea.

"Take me to Roulsville—to my own home.

They'll look there—in the empty house and—
and I won't need to explain."

"Say, she's clever," the workman cried in
honest admiration. "Slip me the beads, partner. She's earned 'em."

"No! No!" Judy cried, "not a bribe. I've
promised. Isn't that enough?"

"The beads will hold you to it."

"No!"

"All right. We'll keep 'em. They cost a
tidy sum at that," the workman drawled. He
reached for the black bag that had been over
Judy's head when she was kidnaped.

"No! No!" she protested again. "I
couldn't stand it. I couldn't breathe."

"But you mustn't see," he insisted hoarsely.
"You know too much already."

"Then let me have a drink first."

"You'll get a drink later. I'll leave the bag
loose and won't gag you if you're sure you
won't holler."

Judy submitted meekly. But if the workman
could have known the angry, resentful thoughts
that were smouldering in her mind, the plans
that were taking shape and the stoic courage
that kept her from revealing them, he would
never have released her.

"You'll lie flat on the floor of the car unless you want to be tied again," the voice of her abductor warned her after he had carried her out of her prison.

A muffled assent came from within the bag. Judy knew she would not have been able to sit in the seat of the car even if they had allowed it and a rug on the floor made it fairly soft. She was actually beginning to feel comfortable, and by the time they reached Roulsville, she was fast asleep.

She awoke with a start and would have cried out when the thin arms of her captor lifted her from the car only he held her mouth so that an outcry was impossible.

As soon as he released her she tore at the bag and fumbled frantically with the string that fastened it over her head. She must, she simply must see the car and its other ghostly occupant before it got away.

CHAPTER VI

HOMECOMING

It was all of five minutes before the stubborn string yielded to Judy's tugging and by that time the car was out of sight. Judy consoled herself with the thought that at least she knew the workman and might be able to learn something that she could tell if she kept close watch.

Just then she was tired of thinking, tired of being brave and, as she opened the door of the empty house, she fairly stumbled in. Her own room was upstairs and she felt too dizzy and weak to climb even the one short flight. Instead, she went to her father's office and poured out a glass of cool, sparkling water from the faucet underneath his medicine closet.

After she had quenched her thirst, she walked slowly over to his chair, paused a moment to pat it, and then settled her back against the soft leather upholstery and let her eyes wander longingly in every corner of this room she loved.

A thin coating of dust was over everything and the room smelled stuffy. But it was home! Indeed, it was almost Heaven after that terrifying night in the swamp. At last Judy was safe, and except for the promises she had made, free.

Sitting in her father's chair, she wondered again what he would have done. "Use your head, Judy girl," that was always his advice, but this time her head had been so dizzy. Perhaps it was all a mistake. Had she been brave or had she been a coward? She had chided Horace so many times but was she, after all, any more courageous than her brother?

"Oh, Dad! Dad!" she told his chair. "If you and Mother were only—here."

Her voice broke and the sentence ended in a sob as she buried her head in her arms and leaned forward on her father's desk.

It was in this position, three hours later, that Horace and her grandfather found her. Exhausted from her night of worry and suspense, she had fallen into a heavy sleep.

"Judy, my poor little sister!" the boy exclaimed tenderly. "Oh, Grandpa, why didn't we think of looking in the house before?"

"Hanged if I know," Mr. Smeed replied, his

voice husky. "Poor girl, she's just plain homesick. Guess Dry Brook Hollow isn't such a fine
place to spend your summers after all."

"That isn't it, Grandpa," Horace replied,
contritely. "It's because Grandma and I
weren't fair. It was a beastly trick taking her
money, but I'll make good. I'll make good,"
he repeated more resolutely as Judy opened her
eyes.

"Oh, you," she murmured dazedly. "I—I
must have been asleep."

"Judy! Sis! I say, will you ever forgive
me? I'm mighty sorry to have made you run
away like this."

Slowly she comprehended the meaning of her
brother's words. That promise! And she
must let them think she had been selfish enough
to run away because she had lost her temper.

She turned a tear-stained face to her broth-
er's anxious one. "It's all right, Horace.
Let's forget it. I want to go back with you and
Grandpa."

"The horses are outside." The old man motioned them to the door.

Fannie and her colt were hitched to a shiny
black carriage. Judy was never sure whether
this vehicle looked old fashioned and funny or

whether it resembled a modern coach, the kind that men with tall silk hats drive through city parks. At any rate, her grandfather insisted that as long as buggies were to be had, he would never trust his feeble hands driving an automobile.

"You must have been lying on the edge of the desk," Horace commented when they were seated in the carriage. "Your face is marked from it."

"From the desk?"

Horace touched her cheek. "Right here, and on the other side, too. It makes you look queer."

"That's where they bound me with that awful blue rag," Judy wanted to say, but she remembered her promise and merely answered, "Does it?" in as indifferent a tone as she could manage.

She noticed that Horace, too, looked queer. His light hair, usually as smooth as a trained seal's, stood out grotesquely where he had passed his fingers through it in nervous agitation. His eyes, too, showed the effects of a sleepless night. Grandfather Smeed also looked unusually pale.

"What did you do?" Judy asked anxiously.

"You didn't telegraph to Dad and Mother?"

"Oh, no," Horace replied. "We were all sure you had gone away of your own accord. Grandmother told us how you asked for money—" He broke off and looked guilty.

"We were hunting through the grove half the night," Mr. Smeed continued. "That was after we found your book there."

"Oh, I must have dropped it." Judy stopped short. She was naturally an outspoken girl and keeping those promises was going to be harder than she realized. She had almost said, "when I saw the shadow."

She caught Horace looking at her quizzically and realized that he was endeavoring to understand the thoughts that she was trying to hide.

They were driving slowly now as they always did when they passed the dam. Judy was glad to find something else to talk about so that her own harassing experiences might be momentarily forgotten. The great white bank of concrete and the deep green water that it kept imprisoned held a peculiar fascination for her.

"Isn't it wonderful," she breathed, "that two such small streams as Dry Brook and Willow Run can supply water enough to make a lake as big as that."

Horace agreed and pointed out two new buildings that had been added to the paper mill. "This first one is the office, I believe."

Grandfather Smeed would have lingered for a while but that Judy's grandmother was waiting anxiously for news of the lost girl.

As soon as the horses came in sight of the house she hurried out on the porch to welcome her. She neither apologized nor scolded but the hot plate of food that was promptly set before Judy was ample proof of her grandmother's sympathy.

The others were glad of a little nourishment too and Mr. Smeed declared that none of them had eaten enough to keep a bird alive since Judy disappeared.

"By the way, Judy, where did you get your supper?" her grandmother asked.

"I—I didn't—have any," the girl confessed.

"Or breakfast either?"

"N-no."

"Child alive!" Mrs. Smeed exclaimed. "You must be starved. It's going on three o'clock."

"Doesn't this look it?" Judy smiled and tried to pass the matter off as a joke as she held out her empty plate for a second helping.

CHAPTER VII

"I'M GOING to ask you to do something very difficult today," Judy told Horace the following Sunday. "Come for a picnic and be my bodyguard. Somebody is apt to steal up behind me and wallop me over the head."

Horace glanced quizzically at his sister. Her voice was more serious than she had intended and it was unlike Judy to be nervous about the woods.

"Are you joking?" he asked in real concern.

"Of course, Silly. What I really want to do is forget all our quarrels and everything else unpleasant and simply give ourselves up to having a good time."

Horace agreed heartily and they promptly set about packing lunch. Mrs. Smeed's pantry always yielded a store of cookies and biscuits and this time a homemade cake. Horace forced it into an oatmeal box and, with sandwiches and fruit, managed to fill a large market basket.

The day was perfect for a picnic. Judy's nightmare experience in the swamp seemed far away and unreal as she and her brother started off. The trees in the beech grove swayed gently and their green leaves glistened in the bright morning sunshine.

As they crossed the bridge over Dry Brook Horace stopped short and pointed.

"Look!" he cried in evident alarm.

For one terrified moment Judy thought he must have seen the shadow, but when she turned in the direction he had indicated she saw at once a less horrible cause for his exclamation. The brook bed was completely dry!

"That is strange," she puzzled. "What do you suppose could have happened?"

"Didn't Grandfather ever tell you the story of Dry Brook?" Horace asked as he and his sister continued along the road and then up a short cut into the woods.

"No, why do they call it that?"

"Well, Judy, it's this way," he explained carefully. "The brook used to go dry every summer. Then one summer about twenty-five years ago it didn't dry up. It hasn't since until today and nobody knows why. Quite a mystery, isn't it?"

Judy eyed her brother shrewdly. "Do you like mysteries?" she asked.

"Sure I do. And to prove it," he added, laughing, "I like my little sister. You're about the biggest mystery I ever came across. One week I come home and find you so mad at me that you have gone off and scared the family half to death and the next week you invite me on a picnic. What do you say we climb up to the top of the hill and have our lunch under those big rocks?"

"Oh, where the stone seats are? I'd love it," she exclaimed, "and after that let's try and find the head of Dry Brook. I would like to see what made it go dry."

"I knew you would," Horace replied with a grin.

They had been picking their way through a dense briar patch, now and then stopping to sample the luscious blackberries that hung from the bushes. Several years previous this part of the woods had been cleared of timber and briars had sprung up in the place of trees that had been transformed into paper in the Roulsville mill. Beyond the briar patch, right on the ridge of the hill, were the rocks. It was still early when they reached them.

"Remember when we built a fire here, Judy?"

Horace peered eagerly into a well remembered cave underneath the tallest rock.

"And you fixed those stones for chairs," his sister continued reminiscently. "See, they're still there. It looks as if other people had been here since."

She picked up a scrap of paper and examined it. "The Farringdon Daily Herald. Does it look familiar?"

"It sure does," Horace replied. "Here's a bit of church news I wrote myself. And on the other side is a big hold-up story."

"Did you write that too?"

He shrugged his shoulders. "Donald Carter always gets the front page news. Why, if I ever was assigned to report a hold-up——"

Words seemed to have failed him. It was simply unthinkable that "Sister," as his fellow reporters called him, should ever write up anything really exciting.

Unthinkable to Horace, the spoiled son of an over-indulgent mother and grandmother but not to his sister.

"We might even make a newspaper story out of Dry Brook's freakish disappearance."

"You're right!" exclaimed Horace, standing up so suddenly that he gave his head a hard rap on the rock that formed the ceiling of the cave. "Gee! I never thought of it but that would be a good story. Now if we can only find the head of Dry Brook."

"Maybe if I climbed upon top of the rock I could see where it is."

Suiting her actions to her words, Judy soon stood outlined against the sky, her lithe body poised as if for flight.

"Look out! You might fall," Horace called from below. The danger of the picture impressed him more than its beauty.

"Oh, I can see for miles," she exclaimed utterly disregarding his warning. "Roulsville looks like a toy town from here and the dam is a tiny white block with a dot of quicksilver spilled above it."

"I thought you were going to look for the head of Dry Brook," Horace reminded her.

She had turned and was gazing at the opposite hill.

"Isn't it wild!" she went on ecstatically. "Why there isn't a house or even a piece of cleared land as far as I can see. I wonder what that white thing is across the valley. Do you suppose you could climb up and tell me?"

"I can see from here." He was standing on
the ledge of rock just below her. "It looks like
a stone quarry. Funny that we never noticed it
before."

"It's been a year since we were up here,"
she reminded him. But still she stood scanning
the opposite hill and wondering. There were
so many mysterious things in Dry Brook Hollow that surely some of them must have something to do with the big mystery that she was
trying to solve—what it was that the workman
meant about the dam and the pit.

"Judy, do you suppose Dry Brook heads over
there?" Horace pointed to a clump of trees,
taller than the others. They were just beyond
the briar patch and to the left where the hill
sloped in two directions. On the farther side
Judy observed a slanting rock with a flash of
silver across it.

"Falling water and that wasn't there before
either," she thought.

"Let's leave our lunch basket here while we
explore," she suggested aloud as she climbed
down from her lofty perch. "We can always
find our way back to this big rock and I do
want to eat in the cave."

Accordingly, they concealed the basket in the cave and started out unencumbered.

"We're sure to find the brook if we keep on going," Horace declared. "We only crossed it once and it must be in this direction."

Judy found it difficult to keep up with him. He seemed inspired by the possible newspaper story and anxious to reach the brook as quickly as possible. In fact, he stumbled over a muddy hollow without even noticing that it extended in a long line on down the hillside.

"What's this?" Judy inquired, stopping short and scrutinizing the ground. "It looks to me as if this might have been a brook—once."

"It does at that," Horace agreed. "Now we can follow it to the spring. What luck!"

It took them in and out among the briars and finally to the very clump of trees that Horace had indicated from the rock.

"This must be it," he said, looking doubtful. "Would you have known it?"

"I certainly wouldn't. I had an idea it would be a pretty place. This looks like a cow path."

Horace laughed. "It is muddy," he agreed.

"It looks as if someone had been digging here," Judy declared as she kicked over a stone with the toe of her shoe.

It was true. The spring certainly had been tampered with. The water was the color of weak tea and the brook itself seemed to disappear almost as suddenly as it had emerged from the rocky bank. A dam of poles and mud packed in between had been constructed just below the spring and water could be heard bubbling under ground. Someone had purposely changed the course of Dry Brook and apparently the underground stream had its outlet on the other side of the hill where Judy had seen the waterfall.

"It's a crime," she cried vehemently. "Grandfather won't have any water for his stock. Besides, I should think it would slow up work at the paper mill if less water flows into the big dam."

"It certainly would," Horace agreed. "Maybe some man with a grudge against the company has done it for revenge."

Immediately Judy thought of the black bearded man with the shovel and his ghostly companion. Could this crude embankment be the dam they were talking about? She felt sure she had hit upon a clue but, because of her promise, she said nothing.

CHAPTER VIII

A DARING PLAN

"THIS spoils my 'freak of nature' newspaper story," Horace remarked gloomily as he surveyed the muddy spring.

And Judy did not deny it. If her abductors had anything to do with it how much better it was for them not to know that their plot had been apprehended. Perhaps, when all the facts were made plain, Horace's "freak of nature" newspaper story would be one of the front page variety. "Angry workmen plot against mill. Secret discovered by young reporter and his sister while on picnic. . . ."

"Come on, Judy," Horace was urging her impatiently. "You're not going to stand there gazing at that dirty water all day."

Judy started back in surprise as she often did when her thoughts were interrupted suddenly. Reluctantly she left the spring and they retraced their steps to the giant rock where they had hidden their lunch.

"You clear a place on the floor," Judy directed as they entered the cave, "and I'll fix the food. I put it right back here. I'm sure I did. Oh, Horace!"

To her dismay the basket was overturned and the fragments of the cake box scattered in all directions. Broken crackers, bread crumbs and a squashed banana were all that was left of their delicious lunch. A big track told the tale.

"Horrors! A bear!" Horace shrieked.

Gray eyes shining, she leaned forward to see. "Oh," she exclaimed in evident disappointment, "only a track."

In spite of his fright, Horace saw humor in the situation and burst out laughing.

"Good thing it was a track. If it had been a real bear you two would have bumped noses. Judy, aren't you afraid of anything?"

"Not much." She was examining the track.

"This is no bear track," she announced presently. "It looks to me like the footprint of a big dog."

"A dog would have to be the size of a horse to make a track like that."

"I know, Horace. But some dogs are almost the size of horses. Charlie Austin's dog, for instance. He buys whole legs of mutton for that beast."

"And who, may I ask, is Charlie Austin?"

Judy looked at her brother in surprise. Then she remembered that he worked in Farringdon and laughed softly. "If you were a girl and lived in Roulsville you wouldn't be asking who Charlie Austin is. He drives a sporty yellow roadster and it is considered a rare privilege to ride beside him. Every girl in high school is sentimental about him. That is, every girl but myself," she added as an afterthought. "I don't fancy his type."

"I'm glad you don't," Horace commended her. "What does this Charlie Austin do for a living? That's the real test."

"I think so too." Judy had a far-away look in her eyes. "That's why I like your being a reporter, Horace. There's so much opportunity. Sometimes I wish I were a boy."

"And you would be——"

"A detective," she broke in quickly. "A great one who goes into all kinds of dangers. I wouldn't mind that—afterwards. There would be that thrill of finding out things. You can't imagine what a satisfaction there is in hitting on a real live clue."

To Horace, Judy was again the mystery girl. He could not know that she was thinking of the

spring in connection with a plot that, somehow, involved people's lives. Perhaps others
were imprisoned in "the pit." Goodness! It
was like one of Poe's horror stories and that
ferocious dog which had barked outside her
prison might be the same dog which had made
the track there in the cave beside them.

"Coming back to earth," Horace said with
a roguish grin. "What does this Charlie Austin do for a living?"

"Oh!" Judy came back to earth with a light
laugh. "Forgive me, Horace. I just will day
dream. But you might know what Charlie
Austin does for a living. He wouldn't have
any but the foremost job in town."

"He's not the new manager of the mill?"

"Exactly. Do you wonder that the girls all
have an eagle eye on him? I suppose there's
something unnatural about me, but once I actually turned down an invitation to go for a
ride in the yellow roadster. I feel safer in
Dad's car or behind Grandpa's horses."

"Good little Judy! I guess Dad is right
when he says he can trust your head."

There was a wistful expression in the boy's
eyes and Judy guessed that he longed for his
father to place the same trust in his son.

"I suppose this Charlie Austin will be at the spelling bee," Horace said presently. "Judy, do you still want to go?"

"Do I still want to!" she exclaimed. "Why, wild horses couldn't keep me from going."

"Wild horses will probably take you there," her brother answered dryly. He was thinking of the colt that Judy insisted on riding. But, as they quit the cave and started for home, she was thinking of something else. Grandmother Smeed had refused to give her a dollar and Judy's pride would not let her ask for it again. Her allowance was gone. She had bought a canary bird of Edna Jenkins and the poor thing had only lived three days. Judy suspected that the storekeeper's daughter knew it was sick when she sold it, but that didn't help solve the problem of a ticket for the spelling bee.

Judy was silent as she and her brother descended the hill carrying the empty market basket. Now and then she stopped, thoughtfully nibbling at a blackberry. There were loads of them on the bushes and a plan was slowly taking shape in Judy's mind. It was a daring plan and one which she could not confide in her brother without breaking a promise.

When they were about half way down the hill it started to rain. One of these sudden summer showers that come without warning and are over in half an hour. Horace walked on ahead and held back the wet bushes but even this consideration helped very little. By 'the time they reached the new cement roadway their clothes were drenched.

"I'm glad I waited with my surprise," he said mysteriously. "It might come in handy."

Judy glanced at her wet feet and remembered that Horace had promised to buy her some shoes in Farringdon. But shoes were nothing to be enthusiastic about, especially the sturdy type of oxford which were the only suitable kind to wear in Dry Brook Hollow.

Soon they came in sight of the house, partly hidden behind trees and everything looked warm and cheerful. The chimney was sending up a straight line of smoke and they would be able to dry themselves by the kitchen fire.

After a supper consisting of lamb stew with vegetables, biscuits and honey from Grandfather's own bee hives, topped off with Grandmother's good apple pie, Horace darted out of the room. When he returned a large tan box was under his arm.

"Better come up in your room where there's a large mirror," he suggested.

"I won't need a mirror to try on shoes."

"Oh, yes you will." Pushing her gently ahead of him, Horace insisted in spite of her protests that she open the box in her own room.

As soon as she had removed the cover she started back with an excited squeal and stood for a moment speechless. All she had expected to find was a pair of serviceable shoes and possibly silk stockings to match, but there in a square fold lay the daintiest, loveliest party dress and, most wonderful of all, a necklace of blue beads fastened together with a slender gold chain. The dress was pale yellow with little sprigs of blue flowers and the beads were a perfect match for it.

"Isn't it gorgeous?" she exclaimed as she held it up. "It looks just as if the wind had blown all those darling little flowers up against a sunset sky. I just love it, Horace."

"It does make you look pretty," he remarked, surveying his sister. "It shows up all the gold in your hair. There's something else in the box, you know."

Judy dived in again and produced a lovely pair of white satin pumps with sheer stockings to match and, at the very bottom, a crisp dollar bill.

"Oh, Horace!" she cried. "You didn't need to give me that. Keep it and buy yourself a ticket. These other beautiful things are enough to give me."

"But you'll need the dollar——"

"Oh, no, I won't," she replied with a proud lift of her chin. "I'm going to sell blackberries and earn my own ticket money."

"Sell blackberries!" Horace exclaimed "How on earth!"

"Oh, ride the colt to Roulsville and simply sell them. That's easy. Grandfather!" she called down the stairs. "May I have the colt on Wednesday?"

"Sure," he replied, "but don't let him break your neck."

Horace looked at his daring sister in astonishment. Inwardly he had fears for her safety if not for her very life.

CHAPTER IX

EARLY Tuesday morning Judy was up and dressed for the woods. Armed with two eight-quart berry pails, she called goodbye to her grandparents and started toward the hill. No one noticed that she also carried a spade and a hoe.

If the task she had set for herself was to be accomplished quickly Judy would need assistance. She hesitated to ask Edna Jenkins as she had shared the secret of the workmen's quarrel.

"But digging is hard work," Judy said to herself, "and Edna is stronger than I am. If only she doesn't ask too many questions! I can pay her by giving her a ticket to the spelling bee."

Edna was up early, waiting on trade while her mother did the morning's housework. The last customer left just as Judy entered, leaving the two girls to themselves.

"I suppose you've come selling tickets to

that spelling bee,'' Edna began. ''Well, you needn't bother. I've got mine.''

''You have!'' This piece of news surely produced the desired effect. ''Why, Edna, I thought you would buy your ticket of me.''

''I didn't buy any ticket,'' Edna pointed out. ''It was given to me by a fellow. I'm going with Charlie Austin in his yellow roadster.''

''You are!''

It seemed incredulous. Edna Jenkins was about the last girl in the world that a conceited young spendthrift like Charlie Austin would be apt to choose. She was neither pretty nor sociable while he was able to mingle with the most charming kind of girls.

''What are you going to wear?'' Judy asked in perplexity. She knew Charlie Austin would expect it to be something that would look well with his own stylish clothes.

''Wait a minute and I'll show you.''

Edna darted out of the rear door and presently returned with a shimmering chiffon dress held aloft on a satin covered hanger.

''Well, how do you like it?'' she inquired.

''Beautiful. I have a new dress too——''

''I'll bet you have,'' Edna interrupted her. ''And I know where you got it.''

"Oh, did Horace tell you?"

"No. Charlie Austin did. Judy, there's no use acting innocent. You're paid to keep quiet, same as I am. There's no one here in the store to overhear what we say."

"What do you mean I'm paid to keep quiet?" Judy flared up hotly. "Edna Jenkins, that isn't true!"

"You can't call me a liar," Edna cried, banging on the counter with both fists. "Charlie told me with his own lips that he had fixed you so you wouldn't talk."

For a moment Judy stood bewildered. But when she grasped the true meaning of Edna's words she decided that the sooner she was out of sight the better. One thing for which she was truly thankful was that she had left the tell-tale spade and hoe outside the front door. Now, if she could leave the store unseen there would be little danger of arousing Edna's suspicion. The dog track and Edna's remarkable disclosure dovetailed perfectly.

Murmuring some kind of an excuse to the storekeeper's daughter, Judy opened the door and stole cautiously down the steps. Once on the main road she broke into a run. Now she knew that her plans were dangerous but, nothing daunted, she meant to carry them to a finish.

"So Charlie Austin himself is the instigator of this plot. Of course that workman wouldn't have money enough to pay all those bribes. He probably kept the necklace——"

Judy's lips curved into a faint smile as she thought of the other necklace, the one her brother had given her. It was less expensive but she wouldn't trade it for a dozen strings of pearls.

"And my promise not to talk doesn't mean much while I can still think and act," Judy continued reasoning. The exact nature of the plot was still something of a puzzle but she knew of a sure way to defeat it.

The spade and hoe were heavy and the berry pails cut into her arm with their wire bails, but Judy dared not hope for any kind of assistance. Horace, the only one whom she could ask to help her, would not be home again until Saturday and that might be too late. Besides, he would be so frightened that he might try to dissuade her if he even suspected that there was danger.

"I'll just have to do it alone," Judy reasoned as she marched resolutely up the hill and into the woods. The climb was a hard one and her arms ached from the weight of the berry pails and tools for digging. She would have let the berry-picking wait until another day but that was her only excuse for coming.

In vain Judy searched the hillside for the taller trees that grew at the head of Dry Brook. She had started up the hill a different way, thinking it would be nearer, but now everything looked unfamiliar. Why, there even was a road.

"I never knew that!" Judy exclaimed as she sat down beside it to rest for a moment. "It's quite a road at that." She bent and examined the ruts more closely. "Somebody has been driving trucks up here. Oh, good heavens!"

There was a rustling sound in the bushes and all at once a long shadow fell across the road. Judy dropped behind a clump of sumacs as silently as a ghost. She glanced at the spade and hoe in the grass beside her.

"Well, at least I can defend myself if that thing sees me," she thought bravely. "This time I don't get carried off without a struggle."

But whatever caused the shadow glided noiselessly by and when Judy dared raise her head again the road was perfectly clear. Still she did not feel that it was altogether safe.

Back in the woods again her courage returned and it was not long before she sighted the big rock where they had found the dog track. Using the two implements she carried as staffs with which to climb, she made her way toward it and then turned in the direction of Dry Brook. She came upon it considerably below the head and followed the stony brook bed to her goal. The plot had worked well, for not a drop of water was left, only dry mud with dead fish caked on the surface. This struck Judy as being particularly horrible. The men who had tried to silence her tongue had also murdered dozens of innocent fish and all, she felt sure, for the sake of revenge. Perhaps someone at the mill had underpaid Charlie, or caused him to lose money. He and his ghostly accomplice were, no doubt, the instigators of the plot and the ones who had paid those two workmen to keep quiet. They might have been the ones who did the digging. Judy Bolton, with the courage of a true heroine, would be the one to undo their revengeful work.

She understood the theory of Dry Brook well enough to know just where and how to begin. First she would dig underneath the

JUDY BOLTON STARTED TO UNDO THE
REVENGEFUL WORK.

The Vanishing Shadow.

artificial dam that the schemers had constructed and then depend on the force of Dry Brook to do the rest.

In spite of the danger of her plan, she found a peculiar joy in watching the imprisoned waters bubble forth as she dug away piece after piece of the muddy embankment. Her arms grew weary and she shifted from spade to hoe to give them a rest.

Suddenly there was a falling of packed earth and a rush of water. Judy sprang to one side and almost lost her footing as Dry Brook raced down the hillside, taking with it the hoe, which she had dropped in her frantic effort to save herself.

The spade she decided to leave behind. Neither of these implements were worth the effort it would take to carry them back to her grandfather's farm.

Exhausted, Judy sank down beside a bush which was loaded with berries. Oh, if they would only fall into her pails without any toil on her part. Then she remembered the lunch she had packed inside one of the berry pails. The dainty sandwiches were refreshing. After they were finished and she had rested a little she was ready to go on with her plan.

All afternoon she picked. There were two eight-quart pails to fill with blackberries and that took time and patience. It grew so dark before she had finished that she found herself picking other things than blackberries. When her fingers closed over a large black beetle she decided it really was about time to go home. The pails were almost full. That evening when she cleaned and measured them there were twelve quarts of large, luscious berries and neither of her grandparents suspected that it had not taken her all day to pick them.

"How much should I charge for them?" she asked.

"Not more than twenty cents a quart," her grandfather answered. "They're asking twenty-five for tame ones at the store."

"Two dollars and forty cents!" she exclaimed after she had finished doing the sum in her head. "Enough and to spare."

"Why did you want it?" Mr. Smeed asked.

"For the spelling bee," she replied. "I thought you knew."

"Bless you! I would have given you a dollar. I'd go myself if it didn't take so much time hauling water for the horses now the brook has gone dry. I'm all fagged out by night."

Judy looked up from her pails of measured berries.

"Dry Brook isn't dry any more," she announced triumphantly.

That was all she dared say until the morning when she planned to ride the colt to Roulsville and sell her blackberries. That, however, was not the only reason for this intended journey. The president of the Roulsville Paper Mill might be interested to know that one of his trusted officials was, in reality, a treacherous criminal.

CHAPTER X

ALMOST before daylight the next morning Judy was out in the stable fixing up the colt for his first long trip as a saddle horse.

She had a little plan of her own for the berry pails. A strap was hooked securely around the bail of each pail and then suspended across the colt's back so that a pail hung on either side of him, the weight of the pails preventing the device from sliding off.

"It looks risky," observed Mrs. Smeed when she saw the clever arrangement. "It might be all right on old Fanny but the colt isn't used to pails dangling at his sides. They're apt to scare him. He will spill your berries, sure."

"I have an idea!" exclaimed the resourceful Judy. "Lend me a couple of kettle covers and we'll clamp them down on the pails and tie them. Then the colt can act up all he pleases and not a berry can get out of the pails."

Mrs. Smeed consented to this plan and after

68

the pails were roped securely to their covers Judy kissed her goodbye, swung herself and her berries over the colt's back and started off. Indeed, she started a little sooner than she intended for the colt could feel the pails bumping against his sides. Away he went at a gallop and the harder he galloped the harder the pails bumped against him.

By the time they reached the main road he had attained the speed of a race horse and Judy was clutching at his mane and screaming "Whoa!" with all her might. He slackened his pace just as Charlie Austin's yellow roadster turned a corner onto the cement and in a flash he was off again.

The long stretch of white cement was being fairly eaten up by the colt's long strides.

They passed the dam, a great white blur across the horizon. They passed the paper mills and their high smoke stacks seemed to be racing by. The railroad! The train!

With a sudden panic-stricken jerk at the reins, Judy attempted to turn the colt. He whirled and reared. She screamed and lost her hold on his mane. The frightened girl felt herself being hurled through space and the berry pails with her.

The ten-fifty whizzed by, its whistle screeching. On a grassy bank not three feet from the railroad track, Judy listened to the grinding of its wheels and realized, with a sinking sensation, that she might have been under them. The colt, freed from the frightening pails, had cut loose and was now galloping for home.

A man in dirty overalls helped Judy to her feet and asked if she was hurt. Dazed by her fall, she leaned back on his shoulder and closed her eyes without answering. Fearing that she had fainted, the man motioned for some of his companions and in a short while a group of men had clustered around, all jabbering in excited voices and trampling over the spilled berries.

"Careful there!" shouted an excited, boyish voice. "Can't you see you're stepping on those blackberries?"

The men moved back obediently and the obliging young fellow who had dismissed them offered to help collect the spilled berries. The others stood and watched for a while and then went quietly away.

"Something to tell their families about when they get home," remarked the young fellow who was helping. "Say, don't I know you?"

Their eyes met suddenly and both of them began to laugh. The boy was Peter Dobbs, grandson of the kind old man who was president of the paper mill. Judy had known Peter well when they were children but since he had been studying law at Farringdon University she had seen little of him.

"And how odd that we should meet today," she exclaimed. "When my chief reason for coming to Roulsville was to see your grandfather. I have a message for him and intended to stop at the mill on my way back to the farm."

"But Grandpa isn't there any more," Peter objected. "Come along with me and you can see him at the house."

"You mean your grandfather isn't president of the mill any longer?" Judy asked in amazement.

"Why, yes. That's exactly what I mean. He's retired, sold his interest in the mill last week."

"And then he can't help me."

Disappointment sounded in Judy's voice. She was walking bravely beside Peter, trying not to limp although her back pained with every step. He had taken both of the refilled pails over one arm and was assisting her with the other.

"How did your grandfather happen to retire?" Judy asked presently.

"He says it was to make a place for younger men," Peter replied. "The new president is Mr. Rubin, a reticent young fellow who turns over most of his work to the office manager."

"You mean to Charlie Austin? Tell me, Peter, what do you think of him?"

"I think he'd make a good collar advertisement," the Dobbs boy replied with feeling. "But personally I'd like to get hold of him by the collar and give him a good shaking. Grandpa would never have sold his share of the business if it hadn't been for that domineering young scoundrel."

"Really!" Judy's eyes were instantly alight. "It was about Charlie Austin that I wanted to see your grandfather. He has been up to something funny and it seemed to me that the company ought to know about it. But now I suppose I'll have to see this Mr. Rubin."

"Maybe I could help you," Peter suggested and Judy, glad of a sympathetic listener, told him about the dam at the head of Dry Brook.

"It looked to me as if it had been done by

someone who wanted to injure the company's business," she finished. "Anyway it was a mean trick on the farmers in Dry Brook Hollow. And I—I dug it out."

Peter gave a surprised whistle. "You did! All by yourself?"

"Yes, all by myself, and now I want the company to know about it."

"Gee!" Peter exclaimed after a long silence. "You're a plucky girl, Judy. Didn't it ever occur to you that thwarting schemes like that one might be dangerous?"

"It never occurred to me that it was anything but dangerous. I like dangerous things. That's why I ride the colt," she added with a laugh.

"But what gave you the idea that Charlie Austin had anything to do with it?"

"His dog track." Judy hesitated. That was all she dared tell without breaking her promise.

They had reached the spacious white house where Peter lived with his grandparents and were turning in at the gate. Judy felt suddenly conscious of her appearance and wanted to leave the berry pails outside.

"What did you intend to do with them?" Peter asked curiously.

"Sell them," she replied briefly. "But no one would want to buy them now. They're so terribly jammed."

"Someone might use them for jam," he suggested and as soon as his grandmother had greeted them and heard Judy's story about the train, he passed the suggestion on to her.

"That's so," she agreed, nodding to Judy. "Jam is a weakness with Peter. How many quarts of berries are here?"

"There were twelve but now they must be more than half gone. The bottom of the pail is full of juice but you couldn't count that."

Mrs. Dobbs had been examining them while Judy talked. She began measuring them by cupfuls into a large preserving kettle.

"They're still clean," she said. "This juice is as clear as can be. The juice has to be pressed out just like that for blackberry jam."

"A queer way to make it," Peter said dryly.

"Now," continued his grandmother, "if you want to sell them they are all ready to go into jam this afternoon. If I give you a dollar for them will it be enough?"

"Quite enough," Judy replied with a grateful smile. "I wanted it to pay for my ticket to the spelling bee. Somebody sent me ten."

"Ho! Ho! Kind of a puzzle who sent them, eh?"

Judy turned around and there, at the door, stood old Mr. Dobbs, fat and jolly, just as she remembered him.

"You gave her a start," Peter chided him. "She's apt to be jumpy after what happened."

"I know," Mr. Dobbs chuckled. "You're the young lady who just missed the ten fifty. It's all over town how she whirled the colt just in the nick of time. They tell me you and your berry pails went flying through the air like a flock of birds. Lucky you're alive, little miss. What happened to the berries?"

"You'll eat them next winter," replied Mrs. Dobbs. "They're on the stove now. Smell them?"

He sniffed and chuckled delightedly. "Aha, Peter. So that's your reward for assisting the fair lady. And how does the headless horseman of Dry Brook Hollow feel by now?"

"I'm all right, if you mean me," answered Judy, laughing. Then her eyes grew suddenly serious. "Tell me, Mr. Dobbs, do you know anything about those tickets? There was the most curious yellow paper inside the envelope and it was marked with a blue cross."

CHAPTER XI

As soon as Judy mentioned the cross Peter began to grin and his grandfather broke into a loud guffaw.

"I told you that would set somebody thinking," he chuckled.

"But what does it mean?" insisted Judy.

Pulling out a drawer in his desk, Mr. Dobbs withdrew a typewritten sheet of paper. "You show her," he directed Peter.

The typewritten sheet, he explained, was the new mailing list. Mr. Dobbs himself had sent out the tickets to everybody, young or old, who seemed to know how to spell. Grade schools, high schools and colleges all were included. There were three crosses opposite three names on the list and one of these names was Judy's own. There were also three small circles.

"Granddad bet on the circles and I bet on the crosses," Peter pointed out. "There are prizes for the three winners."

He handed Judy the sheet of paper and she

examined it carefully to see if any of the chosen winners were people she knew. Peter had bet on his grandfather, a pretty safe bet, Judy thought. And his grandfather had bet on him. The rest, with a single exception, were names of strangers. The exception was old Mr. Roberts, the postmaster.

"The other two are from Farringdon," Peter told her. "You'll meet them Friday night."

"They certainly are royal sounding names." Peter laughed.

"That's Arthur Farringdon-Pett and his sister, Lois. They are descended from the original John Farringdon."

"Who was he? The man who founded the city of Farringdon?"

"Exactly. For a long time they had a large estate that took in all of what is now the fashionable Grove Street section. The estate has been divided since, part of it sold and part given to the city for a park. But the Farringdon-Petts still own the fine old homestead. The house is a big one, not at all like any in Roulsville. It is made of gray stone and has ivy climbing over it and turrets like a castle. There is a wide lawn and a fountain in front

and in back there is a lake with water lilies and
swans——''

"Are you sure you're not making that up?"
questioned Judy, her gray eyes wide with interest. "And if they have a house like that why do
they bother coming to an ordinary spelling bee
in a little town like this?"

"Because they can spell. Can you think of
a better reason?"

Judy confessed that she could not.

Meanwhile Peter's grandmother had been
busy preparing dinner and insisted that Judy
stay and enjoy it with them. Although in comfortable circumstances, Mrs. Dobbs still did her
own cooking. With her it was an art—something to be attempted only by experts. The
inviting table set with tall glasses of iced
lemonade brought back memories of another
Judy with rosy cheeks and windblown hair
who used to race in after a game of tag with
Peter. Horace always came in a little behind
them and, because he needed something to
build him up, usually was offered a second cin-
namon bun with his glass of lemonade. Then
they would stay and see the puppy or Peter's
new goldfish or Checker's kittens.

Checker was the Dobbs cat. Every spring

she obligingly presented them with a new family and, as Peter once said, half the cats in Roulsville could trace their ancestry to old Checker. To Judy's surprise and delight, it was the same cat who now mewed around the table.

"Just what I told you, Grandma," Peter said. "Checker is offended if a guest comes and doesn't see her kittens."

"Maybe she remembers me," Judy laughed. "How I used to love kittens—and still do. Are they very small?"

"Growing up fast. Soon have to be getting rid of them. Take one home if you like," said Peter Dobbs goodnaturedly. "They're much safer pets than that frisky colt."

After dinner was finished and they had chatted over their coffee, Peter led Judy to the familiar stable which had been remodeled to accommodate Mr. Dobbs' car. In one of the old mangers the kittens romped and chased each other's tails. Judy felt like a little girl again as she and Peter romped with them, waving pieces of straw and pretending that their hands under a blanket were mice waiting to be caught.

Afterwards Judy chose the liveliest kitten for her own. He was all black but his feet and the tip of his nose, and Peter said that he looked like a blackberry dipped in sugar.

"Blackberry," she repeated as she stroked the soft ball of fur clinging to her shoulder and holding fast to her dress with his sharp little claws. "Why, that's just the name for the kitten."

"So it is," agreed Peter. "Shall I put him in a box for you?"

"Don't bother," she replied. "It will be easier carrying him like this—on my shoulder. He knows how to hold on, don't you, Blackberry?"

The kitten purred a drowsy reply and soon afterwards Judy shook hands all around and bid her friends goodbye.

"Thank you all so much," she said gratefully. "I will have the kitten to remember how kind you were to me."

"Going so soon?" asked Mrs. Dobbs.

"Yes, and I must hurry."

Judy had almost forgotten her errand at the paper mill. Now, after her friendly visit, she was beginning to dread it. It was all very well to track down mysteries but Judy would have welcomed a vacation from this one. Charlie Austin might even be in the paper mill office in spite of the fact that she had seen him speeding in the other direction two hours earlier. And it would have been so much easier to tell her story to Mr. Dobbs than to this man, Rubin, who was a total stranger.

"Wait a minute! Judy! Wait a minute!"

Peter was gesticulating wildly and calling from the door of the garage.

"What's the idea?" he demanded, after she had returned. "Aren't you going to let a fellow take you home? You can't walk three miles."

"I've done it before," she replied naïvely.

"And I nearly bursted my lungs hollering at you," Peter went on. "Gosh, Judy! When you get to thinking you might as well be in another world. And," he added fiercely, "you will be in another world if you ever become lost in thought in the middle of the street."

"Oh, Peter, I didn't mean it," she told him penitently. "And, really, it's awfully nice of you to take me home. But I'm afraid you'll have a long wait outside the mill. I told you I intended to see this Mr. Rubin."

"I can hold the kitten for you," Peter offered as he helped her in the car. "You would hardly want to take Blackberry into the office of the

Roulsville paper mill, especially since they have that fancy new building with everything strictly up to date.''

"I suppose that was Charlie Austin's idea, too. Peter! Look out!''

Judy clutched madly at his coat sleeve. They were crossing the railroad track. No train was in sight but she felt as if she could see a train almost upon them, just by remembering.

"You're not nervous?'' Peter inquired and she laughed apologetically.

"I know,'' he continued in a sympathetic voice. "I should have slowed down just to relieve your mind. Sometimes I am a little reckless too.''

Now they were nearing the big dam. It loomed suddenly before them like a towering giant and Judy wondered how changing the course of a little brook could affect anything so massive. Beautiful, it seemed, white against the green of the grass, the blue-green of the water and the blue of the sky. Like tiny waterfalls, miniature rivers trickled through and spread themselves over the pasture land below. Cattle and horses were grazing there and after Peter had stopped the car they sat watching them.

The longer they watched the more certain Judy became that one of the horses looked familiar.

"Could that be my colt?" she asked in perplexity. "And if it is, how did he get in that pasture?"

"It's beyond me," Peter replied. "Maybe broke the fence."

Together they climbed through the pasture gate to get a better view of him. There could be no doubt about it, he was the colt. The spatter on his back, like spilled milk, was final proof. He came at once to Judy's low whistle.

"Now you won't need to take me home." She flashed a smile at Peter.

"You're not going to ride the colt!"

"Why not? He'll behave himself now that there are no berry pails to bump into his sides. Gracious. Where's his saddle?"

Peter pointed to a dark object on the grass near the fence. "And I'll bet that's where he got through," he exclaimed. "See those two posts down, right below the dam."

"Oh, yes." Judy secured an end of the colt's bridle to the gate post. "We'll have to get it and saddle the colt before I go into the mill. I may be in a hurry to get home when I come out.

In other words," she laughed, "I may be chased
out if Mr. Rubin doesn't take to me."

To Judy's dismay, as they started across the
pasture, her feet sank, ankle deep, in water.

"Gosh!" exclaimed Peter. "I never knew
there was a swamp below the dam. It didn't
look like a swamp from the road."

All at once a fearful thought came to Judy.
This swamp was familiar. Their steps caused
the same sound that were made by the feet of
her captors as they carried her from the car.
Was there a house, a cave, a pit?

Unmindful of the colt and his lost saddle, she
scanned the grassy space below the dam to find
what she knew must be there—her prison. She
had seen the dam so many times and was so
well acquainted with the land surrounding it
that it seemed almost impossible—and yet——

"Peter, what is that little house? See?"

"That? Oh, that's nothing but the shack the
workmen used for their tools when they were
building the dam. Nothing to get jumpy
about," he assured her.

"But don't they usually take down the shack
when they are finished?"

"Usually, yes, but this time it appears they
didn't. Judy, what *is* the matter?"

Her face had suddenly gone pale. The one window in the tiny building was boarded tightly. Peter wondered at her frantic insistence that they try the door of the shack.

It yielded readily and soon they were standing inside the same dark room where Judy had spent the most harrowing night of her whole life.

The cot was freshly made and a cloak hung over a nail on the wall beside it. Judy touched the cloak and as she did so it came loose and fell, with a whistling sound. Something jarred out of the pocket and rolled, almost as if it had been thrown, across the floor.

Peter and Judy both jumped back with a concurrent cry of alarm. As though fixed in position by an invisible hand, the muzzle of a revolver pointed directly at them.

"It fell from the pocket of that cloak," Judy reasoned doggedly. "It was all an accident— an accident——"

And yet, even after they had left the hut, that black cloak and the sinister weapon haunted her. In her own mind she connected both of them with the shadow who had eluded her in the grove only to become her captor later when she opened her mouth to call out to Horace.

CHAPTER XII

BLACKBERRY VANISHES

"PETER, we should have taken that gun,"
Judy decided after they had recovered the lost
saddle. "I wish you'd go back in the hut and
get it now. Only," she entreated, "please be
careful. I'm almost sure it's loaded."

"But what do you want me to do with it?"
he asked in a puzzled tone.

"Turn it over to the sheriff, Peter. The one
who owns that weapon is a dangerous criminal.
I know what I'm talking about," she reiterated
gravely in answer to his doubtful look. "But
please don't ask questions. Just tell the sheriff
exactly where you found it and how."

"And I'll probably get jailed myself for
carrying firearms without a permit," Peter
prophesied as he turned back toward the hut.

Judy watched him with fear clutching at her
heart. Suppose the shadow man returned
while they were still there. Oh, what could be
taking Peter so long? She decided to go back
to the hut herself and find out.

Just at that moment Peter emerged carrying something besides the revolver. He held in his hand a blue gingham rag and in the center were three small blood stains.

"It looked suspicious so I thought I'd take it along to the sheriff too," he explained as he exhibited his find.

The very sight of it made Judy shudder. The three blood stains, she knew, must be where it had been bound too tightly across her mouth and caused her lips to bleed. Now the promise bound her lips as surely as had the blue gingham rag.

"It does look suspicious," she agreed. "And the sooner you get it in the hands of the police, the better. I have the colt to take me home now and you won't need to wait."

"In other words, here's your hat——"

"No, Peter. But this may be important. We may be saving somebody's life by gaining possession of this gun. Please go—and hurry!"

"Gosh, Judy," Peter exclaimed as he transferred the kitten from his own arms to hers. "I never knew you to be so serious before. I'll go. Guess I'd go jump in the lake if you asked me to with that look in your eyes. So long! See you next Saturday at the spelling bee."

Halfway to the car he turned and called back, "Remember now, I'm betting on you."

Smiling, Judy assured him that she would spell her hardest and stood watching Peter until the car was out of sight.

"I'd forgotten how nice he was," she thought. Just then she had forgotten something else too, the unpleasant duty of calling on Mr. Rubin and telling him all that she dared tell of Charlie Austin's plot. The colt's impatient whinnying reminded her.

Peter had helped her saddle him. She made sure that he was securely tied and then, mustering all her courage, she walked boldly up to the office of the Roulsville paper mill.

Blackberry, of course, had to be left outside and Judy could think of nothing better to do with him than to drop him into an empty barrel that stood beside the door. There he might mew but he could not possibly get away.

"Is Mr. Rubin in?" asked Judy timidly of Miss Hoyt, the girl at the information desk.

The girl eyed her critically. They had known each other in high school and to know Gladys Hoyt was to dislike her.

"What do you want of him?" she asked shortly. "Some business of your father's?"

"No. My father is out of town. It's a little matter of my own, very personal."

There ensued an awkward moment of silence. Gladys had an unkind habit of scrutinizing people.

"Mr. Rubin has specifically requested that I let no one enter his office unless they are willing to state their errand."

"It's about Charlie Austin," Judy explained. "He has a plan I wanted to discuss with him."

"Oh, I see." There was a withering tone to the girl's voice that made Judy feel about the size of a mosquito. "You just be seated right here, and Mr. Austin will be in presently to look after the matter himself."

"Never mind!" cried Judy in alarm. "It isn't important."

"You'd better wait. The matter may be very important to us."

"Then why can't I see Mr. Rubin?"

"Because our office manager takes care of everything."

That was final. Judy knew there was no use arguing. Her only chance was to slip out of the door while the girl's back was turned.

She waited uneasily on the bench, watching her chances, but Gladys Hoyt had the eyes of a cat. Presently the office telephone rang and as she turned to answer it Judy darted out of the door. Now if the colt would only take her home as fast as he had brought her perhaps she could manage to avoid meeting Charlie Austin.

Too late! The yellow roadster stood parked on the cement road and Charlie himself appeared suddenly and started in the direction of the paper mill office. Judy had not seen him alight from the car but he might have stepped directly out of a bandbox to judge from his tailored appearance. He wore a gray fedora hat perched jauntily on his shining black hair and his gloves and spats were of matching gray. His big dog, adorned with an elaborate collar that must have been made to order to fit his thick neck, followed at his heels.

"Well, just look who's here," he exclaimed the instant he saw Judy. "I suppose you came to see me. Awfully sorry I happened to be out. Didn't the girl tell you to wait?"

"Why—er—yes," Judy stammered. "But I didn't come to see you. I came after my kitten, Mr. Austin."

"A kitten! Why, my dear Miss Bolton, what would we be doing with your kitten?"

"You wouldn't . . . I mean, you didn't."

Judy glanced helplessly in the direction of the barrel. "It was crying—the kitten was. Peter Dobbs gave it to me and it got away."

"Oh, I see." Charlie Austin lifted his eyebrows in amused comprehension. "Perhaps I can help you find it—or the dog." He whistled to the beast at his feet. "Cats! Caesar! Cats!"

"He'll hurt it," Judy cried in alarm as the dog crouched with tail motionless, growling and showing its teeth. "Let me look, won't you?"

"Why certainly," he replied with exaggerated politeness. "And I will gladly help you. Just where may we expect to find your—er—kitten?"

"Oh, anywhere! You can look in the bushes if you like. I'll hunt behind this barrel."

Glad of an excuse to get away from Charlie Austin's close scrutiny, Judy darted toward the barrel where she had hidden Blackberry. She lifted the lid and reached eagerly for the soft ball of a kitten. Instead, her hand touched only the empty interior of the barrel. Blackberry had disappeared.

Charlie Austin, who did not seem to take Judy's lost kitten story very seriously, stood watching with a mocking smile on his lips.

"Hardly expected to find it in a barrel, Miss Bolton, did you?"

She straightened and flashed back at him. "Yes, Mr. Austin, I did. In fact, I felt almost sure I would find it there."

"Sorry not to have been able to accommodate you." He paused and lit a cigarette, then flipped the burned match in the direction of the empty barrel. "I would advise you the next time you decide to call at a business office not to encumber yourself with cats. It may be dangerous."

"I'm not afraid of danger," Judy replied coldly. "The colt is tired of waiting and I must be going now. If you see the kitten——"

"Oh, certainly. I shall return it to its mistress at once. Good day, Miss Bolton."

With heavy heart, Judy turned toward home without her kitten. She untied the colt and threw herself over the saddle. A dozen times on the way home she asked herself, "What could have happened to him?" And a dozen times the question remained unanswered in her mind—except that the shadow . . .

No! She dismissed the thought instantly. It was altogether unreasonable and absurd.

"If I'm not careful," she chided herself,

"I'll have as many imaginary fears as Horace.
I wonder what he would think if he knew."

She decided not to tell him anything about
her experience with the train. For what
seemed ages she had been trying to convince
her brother that the colt was safe. Once he had
the animal under control Judy hoped it would
help him conquer some of his other fears. Of
course, if she kept the story from Horace she
must keep it from her grandparents too.

When Judy arrived at the farm the first thing
Mrs. Smeed wanted to know was what she did
about her lunch.

"I had plenty," her granddaughter assured
her. "Remember Mrs. Dobbs and Peter, the
boy Horace and I used to play with? Well, she
bought my berries and afterwards invited me
to lunch. Mr. Dobbs is the one who sent me
those tickets to the spelling bee."

"It's good to hear that," Mrs. Smeed said
in evident relief. "I had a bite packed for you
but you didn't hear me call. Did the colt gallop all the way to Roulsville?"

"Did he!" she exclaimed. "You should
have seen him. You were right about the pails
frightening him. But he was as good as gold
coming home."

That was all Judy said about her wild ride, but when her grandfather came in from the fields he had to hear the story all over again and this time Judy added a bit about the kitten.

"Peter Dobbs gave him to me," she explained. "He offered to put him in a box but I wanted to carry him. He cuddled into my neck and clung with his paws, just like a baby. Then," she finished brokenly, "he got away. I—I don't know what happened to him."

"Maybe someone else picked him up," suggested Mr. Smeed. Then his face suddenly clouded.

"So you did all that to get a dollar to go to the spelling bee? Why didn't you tell me? I would have given you a dollar."

"So would Horace. But I made him keep it for himself. He's coming up on the train and he will be looking for me. Peter Dobbs will be there too and the Farringdon-Petts and a lot of nice people from Farringdon. Oh! It's going to be a simply glorious party. I can hardly wait."

Her grandfather's face was still solemn.

"Hang it all!" he ejaculated, rising to his feet. "I've got to use the horses all day Friday. Helping Sam Tucker hay it way down below Roulsville. I can't possibly get back in time to take you.''

"Fanny and the colt both?'' she asked anxiously. "Oh dear, Grandpa, I wish you had a car.''

"His hand isn't steady enough to drive one,'' Mrs. Smeed put in. "I guess you'll just have to make the best of it and stay home.''

Stay home when Peter was betting on her!

"If Grandfather can't take me, then I'll walk,'' she announced with determination.

CHAPTER XIII

ARTHUR FARRINGDON-PETT was feeling a bit uneasy. His sky blue sedan, nicknamed Bluebird, had just plowed through an uncomfortable detour where a new bridge was under construction. He had noticed, to his dismay, that Dry Brook was higher than it had been since spring. Earlier in the week the brook bed had been empty and Arthur felt reasonably safe in bringing his sister and their friends into Roulsville.

Lois was always wanting to go to parties that were unique and original. She sat in the rear seat chatting with Donald Carter unmindful of her brother's anxiety. Lorraine Lee, sitting beside him, noticed a troubled expression cross his face.

"What is it?" she asked. "More detours?"

"Oh no," he assured her, trying to laugh off his apprehensive mood, "we're in for a long spin down this new road, and will not have

another detour until we reach Roulsville."
They had passed several farms, and were en-
tering a wooded stretch of land where there
were few houses.

Suddenly Lorraine pointed ahead. "What's
that bit of yellow, Arthur? It looks like a girl
walking."

"So it is," he exclaimed, slowing up the car.
"She must be in for quite a hike in this wilder-
ness. Let's offer her a ride."

"People don't do that," Lorraine objected
with a disdainful toss of her yellow curls.

"Some people do," he returned with a laugh.

"Go ahead! Give her a lift," called Donald
Carter from behind him and Lois added with
enthusiasm. "She can sit next to me."

The slim figure in yellow walking along beside the road certainly made a pretty picture.
She appeared to be dressed for a party except
that she wore sturdy walking shoes. In her
hand she carried a dainty slipper bag which she
swung back and forth as she strode on. She
turned startled gray eyes in the direction of
Arthur's car as he drew it to a stop.

"Going far?" he called out to her.

"Only to Roulsville. I can walk, thank you."

"But," he insisted, "that's a good three

miles and you'll be all tired out for the party. I take it you're going to a party. You're Dr. Bolton's daughter, aren't you?"

"Why yes," she answered in a more friendly tone. "Have you met me before?"

"Sorry, but I haven't had the pleasure. I've merely admired you from a distance. I'm Arthur Farringdon-Pett and this is my sister, Lois, in the back seat. The boy next to her is Donald Carter." Judy at once recognized "the reporter who gets all the front page news" from her brother's description. "And," Arthur continued, "this beautiful damsel beside me is the fair Lorraine. Perhaps you've heard of her."

"Lorraine Lee!" Judy exclaimed, smiling at her. "Why of course. My brother, Horace, works for your father's paper.

"Oh, you mean Sister," the beautiful Lorraine replied pointedly.

"Lorraine!" Arthur reprimanded her sharply.

"Well, everybody calls him 'Sister.' "

Judy's face clouded. She was still standing in the road beside the car. "I—I guess I'd rather not ride," she faltered. "It's pleasant walking."

"It won't be unpleasant riding," Arthur promised.

Lorraine Lee sat silent, disapproval written in the haughty tilt of her proud chin.

Lois, leaning forward, said in a low voice. "Please come. I want you." There was sympathy in her dark eyes and Judy instantly liked her.

"I'll not be intruding?" she questioned.

Lois laughed. "No indeed. Donald is as anxious to make new friends as I am. He has heard Horace speak of you a great many times and both of us feel almost as if we knew you."

"And I'll bet you were on your way to the spelling bee," Donald Carter put in.

"You're one hundred per cent right," laughed Judy as she sank into the luxurious cushions in the back seat of Arthur's car. "And now I won't have to walk."

"And you will have all your surplus energy left for dancing," Arthur suggested from the driver's seat.

"Dancing and spelling," she corrected him and smiled softly to herself. Yes, it was going to be a wonderful party. Now she was sure of it.

They were out of the stretch of woods and

were speeding on toward Roulsville. The tall smoke stacks of the paper mill and the gigantic white dam loomed in sight. Below it was the hut with the door standing wide open.

"We'll be a little early, won't we?" asked Donald Carter. "Or are you going to stop at the mill again?"

"I am going to stop," Arthur answered with a note of firmness in his voice. "There's a light in the office and either Rubin or Charlie Austin must be there. I intend to keep after those birds until they listen to me. How would you girls like to have a soda while you're waiting? There's a combination drug store and everything else right near the paper mill office."

Judy could not suppress a little squeal. Alone with Lois she meant to find out all that she could about her brother's business with Charlie Austin. She was delighted to learn that Lorraine had decided to accompany the boys.

The girls found a table in a far corner of the store where they could be alone and talk. Judy was beginning to feel as if she had known Lois a long time.

"I'm so glad we met you," the dark haired

girl was saying. "Now we can all go to the
spelling bee together."

"That might spoil things for Lorraine,"
Judy confided. "I know she doesn't like me."

"She'll get over that," prophesied Lois in a
low tone. "It's just because she thought it
wasn't proper for Arthur to offer you a ride.
Usually she's a model of good behavior. I
never knew her to say anything so rude. It
hurt me too because I'm fond of her. We've
been playmates since our nurses took us riding
together in our baby carriages."

"I wouldn't want to start a misunderstand-
ing. Perhaps I shouldn't have come."

"Of course you should," Lois assured her.
"Arthur wouldn't have asked you if it hadn't
been all right."

"Tell me," Judy leaned forward and touched
her arm, "why does your brother want to see
Charlie Austin?"

"Something about the dam," Lois answered,
sipping her soda. "He has always been interested in it. He is an engineer and wanted the
contract to build it. It would have been a wonderful opportunity for him but the officials of
the company didn't want to let the contract to
a boy just out of college. There was quite a

little dispute about it and the construction company bid so low that Arthur suspects there was something crooked about the way that dam was built.''

"What dam? The big one?''

Lois laughed. "Of course. You don't know of any other dam, do you?''

Yes, Judy did know of another dam, that small one at the head of Dry Brook. She had felt so sure of herself when she dug it out but now she was beginning to wish that she hadn't gone ahead so hastily with a plan she only half understood. If the big dam wasn't safe then there might have been a good reason for checking Dry Brook. But Charlie Austin had done it—and bribed people to keep still about it—There couldn't have been a very good reason. She decided to try and forget it until after the spelling bee. When the boys returned she ventured only one question.

"Did he have a black kitten with a white nose and white feet?''

"Who? Charlie Austin? Did Charlie Austin have a kitten? Why do you ask?''

"Oh, I lost one,'' she replied. "It disappeared somewhere near the mill and I thought he might have found it.''

Donald Carter laughed loudly. "I can just imagine Charlie Austin playing guardian to a stray kitten!"

"Was he very ugly?" Lois asked anxiously.

"Oh no," the boys replied in mock unconcern. "Only threatened to sic his dog on us. Finally told us to clear out or he would fill us full of bullets. A pleasant chap, I must say."

"Good heavens! What did Lorraine do?"

"I didn't go with them," she replied loftily. "I had quite a pleasant stroll by myself."

CHAPTER XIV

THE SPELLING BEE

ARTHUR turned his long blue car up the road that wound in and out among the trees in Roulsville's pretty hillside park. It was quite a climb to the pavilion but when they reached it Judy could not suppress a squeal of delight. Streamers of blue and yellow crêpe paper were suspended from the ceiling to the pillars of the round building giving it the appearance of a huge Maypole under a canopy.

"Your colors," whispered Lois to Judy as they entered. Lorraine Lee hung behind, sulking because of Judy's presence.

"You look so pretty," Lois went on. "Just as if the whole pavilion had been decorated on purpose for you."

The crowd had not begun to arrive but over in a far corner sat the postmaster and old Mr. Dobbs, together with four or five other gray haired champions of the long ago.

"There's Mr. Dobbs," observed Judy. "He used to be president of the mill. Let's go

104

over and have a little social chat with him."

"Oh yes," replied Lois. "He's the man who wanted Arthur to have the contract but Rubin and all the others opposed him."

"Well, if it isn't the little lady of the blackberry patch!" exclaimed Mr. Dobbs as Judy approached. "How's the frisky colt?"

Peter Dobbs was there too.

"How do you do!" he exclaimed, rushing forward to greet her. "Done any more riding on that demon Pegasus?"

"Not lately," she laughed. "I've been too busy. Almost read the whole dictionary so I'd have a chance to win tonight."

Peter grinned his satisfaction. "Here's hoping! By the way, how's Blackberry?"

"I wish I knew!"

Judy felt suddenly as if she wanted to cry. If she could only forget Blackberry for the evening! After all, she tried to reason, he was only a kitten. Shaking her head and suddenly tilting it high, she resolved to dismiss all unpleasantness and let nothing prevent her from having the time of her life.

Peter, sensing her mood, suggested a dance and they were almost the first couple on the floor. The orchestra had just started playing

but by the time Horace had arrived from Farringdon, his sister was the center of an admir-
ing group of boys, each wanting to dance with
her. She swung around, this time on Arthur's
arm, and let all her worries float away on a lazy
tune.

"And I'm counting on her to win first prize,"
Peter was telling a friend.

Arthur was counting on her too. They all
were. That, and not the prize itself, was the
important thing.

"Come, girls," Arthur summoned. "They're
forming in line."

Judy grabbed Lois' hand and, forgetting
Lorraine, the two stood whispering, waiting for
the contest to begin.

Professor Jaeger, principal of the Roulsville
High School, had been appointed to pronounce
the words. A shiver of expectation ran down
the line as he produced a typewritten page.

"The first words are always easy," Arthur
told them in a loud whisper. "The grade
school children get in on this."

Edna Jenkins, who had come alone, was the
first to go down. Others followed in quick suc-
cession. Professor Jaeger took a fresh sheet
of paper.

"That finishes the easy words," remarked Arthur.

"No talking in the line," spoke the professor sharply. "Tend strictly to your spelling. From now on, whispering will disqualify the contestant."

This was getting serious. Somebody went down on nearly every other word. The postmaster stood proudly at one end of the line, old Mr. Dobbs and his grandson standing at the other and spelling for all they were worth. Donald Carter tripped up on *ptomaine* but Judy spelled it correctly and kept her place. Horace, shoulders squared, was beginning to show a little self respect as difficult words rolled glibly off his tongue. Lorraine Lee stood beside him, spelling with head held high. Lois hesitated, spelled *somersault* with two *m's* and went down. A high school girl near the end of the line got a bad nose bleed and asked to be excused.

"If you leave the line you must be disqualified," said the professor sternly. So the girl spelled for a little while longer with a handkerchief held to her nose. Then she missed and ran for the washbasin. Judy's eyes followed her sympathetically.

The professor lay down the second sheet of paper.

"That finishes the list," he announced. "Now we shall see what we can find in the dictionary."

He took up a fat green book that looked strangely familiar to Judy. He had started with the a's and was going right through, choosing the most difficult words he could find. The pupils left the line, one by one, but the difficult words the professor was choosing were the very ones Judy had picked to study.

Three more people, including Horace, missed on *chlamys* and the postmaster paused for fully a minute before he spelled it right. One of the students misspelled *cochineal*. Peter paused, frowned, spelled it right and kept his place.

The professor appeared worried. Judy heard one of the spectators say there would be little time left for dancing. He skipped over a few pages and went on. Arthur, Peter and two others all missed *syzygy* but Judy spelled it correctly. She was startled when some of the spectators clapped.

The professor rapped on the back of his chair with a ruler. "Save your applause until we are finished, if you please!" he said.

A little of Judy's self-confidence left her when the boys took their seats, but the words were clear in her memory and one after another she spelled them. Then came the word *tsetse*, pronounced as if it ended in an *a*. The postmaster paused, hung his head for a moment and spelled it the way it was pronounced.

Mr. Dobbs chuckled and winked at Judy. A gasp was heard around the room as she spelled the word correctly. The postmaster had gone down while two people were left standing!

For a long time old Mr. Dobbs and Judy stood there spelling. Voices were heard to whisper, "They'll make it a tie."

Then Professor Jaeger tried a little trick of his own. He turned the pages back and began pronouncing words that started with *t*.

"*Tablature, taciturn, ptarmigan.*"

He thought that would trick somebody, and it did. Mr. Dobbs started to spell *ptarmigan* with a *t*. Then Judy, who remembered the bird and its picture under *p's* in her own dictionary, spelled *ptarmigan* as it should be spelled.

A thunder of applause greeted her from every corner of the hall. The professor rapped with his ruler. He rapped and rapped but they would not be quiet. Judy Bolton, a fifteen year old high school girl, had outspelled the best spellers in the county. Judy had won first prize while old Mr. Dobbs had to be content with second. The postmaster, who had won either first or second prize every year for the last seven years, came in for third award, a five pound box of candy which soon disappeared after he had generously passed it all around.

Judy, blushing and smiling, stepped forward to receive the small blue box that Professor Jaeger held out to her. Friends and strangers rushed forward to congratulate her before she had a minute to open it.

"Won't Mrs. Dobbs be pleased when I tell her?" old Mr. Dobbs was saying. "She hoped that you would win it all the time."

"Yes," replied Judy, "and I have her to thank. She bought my blackberries or maybe I couldn't have come."

Peter's eyes were shining. "I knew you could do it," he declared and Judy felt so glad that she had not failed him.

Lois held on to Judy's hand through all the excitement and finally managed to draw her to a corner where, together, they took a peep at the prize.

"Ten dollars in gold!" exclaimed Lois.

EVERY BOY IN THE HALL WAS ANXIOUS TO DANCE
WITH JUDY

The Vanishing Shadow.

"And Mr. Dobbs probably got five. What are you going to do with it?"

Judy was silent, wondering what ten dollars would buy. If she had her way it would be a party, maybe on her birthday, with lights and streamers like tonight. She would invite Peter, Arthur, Lois, Donald Carter and Lorraine, if she would come.

Later, when they were dancing, Arthur told her that Lorraine's father had called for her and she had gone without even bidding anyone goodbye.

Judy was being whirled around and around. Every boy in the hall was anxious to dance with the winner. She felt dizzy with excitement and hardly knew what was happening, only that somebody came to claim every dance.

Then, in a pause between dances, she surprised Edna Jenkins staring at her. Judy had been having such a wonderful time that she had forgotten even to speak to the storekeeper's daughter. Suddenly she felt sorry for Edna, sitting there all dressed in her new clothes and not dancing.

"My dance?" said Arthur, interrupting her thoughts.

"Oh! Do me a favor. Dance with a friend

of mine instead." She led him over to where
Edna was sitting.

Presently she wished she hadn't done it.
Poor Arthur's feet must be suffering while she
and Donald Carter enjoyed the dance.

Arthur came back shortly to scold her.
"What were you doing? Teasing me?"

Judy laughed. "Didn't you like her? She's
Charlie Austin's new girl friend."

"So she told me. Wondered why he hadn't
called for her. It seems he had some important
business to look after at the mill. I'd give a
whole lot to know exactly what that business
could be."

"So would I."

Judy spoke so seriously that Arthur drew
her aside in a secluded corner of the hall.

"You know something more about this affair,
don't you?" he asked.

"No," she replied truthfully. "I'm like you
and merely suspect. But I'm willing to help
you find out as much as you can. I've been
through the woods hunting for clues myself."

"Find any?"

"Plenty," she replied. "For one thing there
was an old road that looked as if heavy truck-
ing had been done along it just recently."

"You don't say!" Arthur's eyes kindled with interest. "You couldn't have found a more important clue. Do you think you could show me just where that road hits the cement?"

"I'm afraid I couldn't," Judy confessed. "You see, I was already in the woods when I found it, but it must be somewhere near the Jenkins' store. Why do you think the road is so important?"

"Because," Arthur answered slowly, "it may lead to the pit."

"The pit!" gasped Judy. And for a moment that was all she could say. She was thinking of the hut where she had been imprisoned. Finally she put the question, "what do you know about the pit?"

"Precious little." His eyes narrowed. "But you look as if you knew a great deal. If you can tell me where they got that sand——"

"Sand?" Judy questioned. "What sand?"

"The sand they used to build the dam."

"Oh!" Light began to dawn upon Judy. So the pit was only a sand pit and she had been thinking of a dungeon. How utterly ridiculous! They couldn't have meant what they said about killing people then. Perhaps they were only trying to scare her. She would have given almost anything in exchange for the privilege of telling Arthur. But she would not break her pledged word of honor. Instead, she only said. "I know precious little too."

"But you said you found plenty of clues."

"I did. There was a dog track that looked big enough to be the footprint of Charlie Austin's dog. And someone had been digging at the head of Dry Brook. There was a little dam. I suppose you noticed that earlier in the week Dry Brook was dry——"

"Yes, and I thanked Heaven for it."

"Why?"

"Because that brook is dangerous——"

"Say, Arthur," Peter Dobbs interrupted, seizing Judy by the arm. "You can't monopolize the prettiest and cleverest girl in the room all night. Dance with me, Judy?"

"But Arthur was telling me——"

"That's all right," he assured her. "You can hear the rest on your way home. I'll take you in my car, if I may."

"You were looking too serious," Peter told her when they were dancing again. "This isn't anybody's funeral. It's a party."

"I know. And the nicest party I ever attended." Judy soon laughed off her anxious mood and her thoughts were caught up in the gay whirl of music.

The party lasted until nearly two o'clock while Horace looked on, always the center of an eager group discussing his sister. They had forgotten all about teasing him, and, best of all, he had forgotten to be shy and self-conscious.

"Gee! I feel proud of her," he kept exclaiming as the boys gathered around him.

"I hoped Judy would win," declared Peter. "She's a pretty safe girl to bet on. So long, boys. I'm off to steal the last dance with her."

"No you don't!" a chorus of voices protested. Judy was smiling at them teasingly. She had already swung into step with Arthur.

CHAPTER XV

STILL wide awake and unbelievably happy, Judy settled herself in the front seat of Arthur's luxurious car. The world was bathed in pale yellow moonlight and the road up Dry Brook Hollow stretched on and on. Judy felt as if she could ride like that forever—away on a white road out into the night. She tossed back her head and let the swift breeze play through her auburn hair.

The others were talking but Judy just sat still, too filled with ecstasy to listen until she detected a note of seriousness in their voices and Arthur brought the car to a full stop.

"See," he said, pointing to the dam which loomed ghastly white in the moonlight, "those cracks are even more conspicuous at night. They seem to be widening by the hour."

"They do seem to be," spoke up Donald Carter from the back seat where he sat with Lois and Judy's brother. "But, of course, that may be only our imagination. Charlie Austin is so

cock-sure it's safe. 'The engineer who built
that dam knew his business' seems to be his pet
argument. By the way, who was the engineer?''

"Someone called Christopher White. At
least that's the name that was signed on the
papers.''

Judy sat forward with a start as Arthur
mentioned the same name that had been on the
torn envelope she had found in the shack. The
spelling bee, the music, the lights, even her
prize were momentarily forgotten.

"I watched them building that dam," Arthur
continued, "and suspected crooked work from
the very first. A man at the gravel works told
me they hadn't bought any sand and, by putting
two and two together, I figured that they must
have used cheap materials in order to make
such a low bid. What you just told me, Judy,
confirms that suspicion. There's an old sand
pit somewhere in these hills but the sand isn't
fit to build roads with, let alone dams. Why,
the safety of everybody in Roulsville depends
on the strength of that concrete. What's more,
the excavation at the base of the dam wasn't
half deep enough. I'll bet water is undermin-
ing that structure even now, and if I'm not very

much mistaken that's the cause of those three large cracks you see.''

"Sounds logical," put in Donald, "but if your theory is true, then what?"

"Then the dam would break and flood the whole valley!"

"Goodness!" exclaimed Judy, after a tense silence. "And all because they used poor sand. I wonder if that white place on the hillside that we thought was a stone quarry could have been a sand pit. Remember, Horace?"

But her brother did not answer. Judy glanced back at him and surprised a look of abject horror on his face.

"You're frightening Horace," she said in a low voice. "Couldn't we wait to talk about the dam? He—he hasn't been well." She felt it her duty to apologize for his weakness.

"I wish I could frighten a few more people," Arthur returned vehemently.

"I know. But not tonight. There are so many pleasant things to talk about. I'm going to plan a party with my prize money——"

"Don't do it," Lois interposed from the back seat. "If what Arthur says is true this spelling bee is probably the last party we will ever attend in Roulsville. We wouldn't have come to this one only he thought the brook had gone dry."

"What did that have to do with it?" Judy asked in alarm.

"Can't you see?" Arthur returned impatiently. "Dry Brook supplies half the water for the mill pond. Just now the stream above the dam is as high as it usually is in April. One more heavy rain storm and the water-level would be raised to a danger point. Those three cracks might split open and flood the town before anybody knew what was happening. Homes would be washed away and Roulsville would be devastated."

"And the people!" gasped Horace, his eyes almost popping out of his head, "what of the people?"

"They would all be killed," said Arthur grimly. "Nothing short of a miracle could save them."

Judy could not quite convince herself that Arthur meant all these terrible things he had been saying. To be sure they sounded logical and dove-tailed perfectly with what she had learned from the workmen's conversation but just then she felt more shame for her brother's cowardice than fear for her own safety.

"Would it have to rain again before the dam broke?" asked Lois who seemed to have perfect confidence in her brother's opinions.

"It might break at any moment," he declared. "I am certain of that. Whether it will take five years or five minutes——"

"Hadn't we better be starting?" asked Horace suddenly. He could not wait for Arthur to finish another lengthy explanation.

"That's right," agreed Donald. "We're below the dam now."

Whether or not he was teasing Horace Judy could not tell.

"Yes indeed," returned Arthur. "A fellow takes his life in his hands every time he comes into Roulsville."

There could be no doubt about the seriousness of this remark. But Judy still clung to her determination not to let anything spoil her good time. Once the car was on its way again she decided to do something to put a little life in the party.

"Isn't this breeze wonderful?" she exclaimed. "Come, let's sing something. Something real lively and gay."

"One of the school songs," suggested Lois, "because we all know them."

The boy and girl voices mingled and, to all appearances, gloom had been dispelled and the dam forgotten. They were singing and laughing and once more Judy wished that Saturday evening would last forever. She told Arthur so.

"Well," he laughed. "It has lasted well into Sunday morning."

Lois, in the back seat, was blinking drowsily. Her head rested on Donald's shoulder and Judy thought how pretty she looked with her dark lashes resting on her cheeks.

All at once Arthur jammed on the brakes. Lois sat up with a start and they all leaned forward to see what had happened.

"Something in the road," he explained. "Guess I didn't hit it, but we'd better look."

"Why Arthur!" Donald exclaimed. "It was only a shadow."

"There it is now!" cried Judy, standing up in the car and pointing. "It's gone past us but please, please follow it."

The driver of the sky blue sedan stared at her incredulously. "And why, my dear girl, do you insist that I follow a shadow at two o'clock in the morning?"

"If you want to find out something real about the dam you will do as I ask," she implored.

"That shadow man is at the bottom of all the crooked work. I feel sure of it. If we could only see his face—identify him. Hurry, Arthur, or he'll be gone."

To Arthur Farringdon-Pett, the practical engineer, Judy's words sounded utterly absurd. But the appeal in her serious gray eyes caused him to turn his car back toward Roulsville.

"We should have overtaken him by now," he remarked after five minutes of driving.

Judy remembered his uncanny habit of disappearing and scanned the bushes at the side of the road. All at once a shadowy shape could be seen moving along ahead of them.

"Why, he's on a bicycle," Arthur exclaimed. "I'll drive slowly so that you can see him."

"He looks like a skeleton," Lois said with a shudder.

All of them could see his back distinctly. He wore a flowing black cloak, the same cloak that had frightened Judy in the little hut when she and Peter were exploring. It was not the cloak, however, that gave him the unreal appearance. It was the fact that his head was bare, absolutely bare of either hat or hair! If it had been a skull the appearance that it presented could not have been any more horrible.

A chill of fear crept over Judy. To think that she had actually been held and touched by the hands of this awful thing. Oh, if she could only tell Arthur! He would know the meaning of the workman's words, "if you lock her up there she'll be killed along with the rest of them." Judy knew now—after she had dug out the dam. Could Charlie Austin have been trying to save lives? Could she have misjudged him? If so, why had he bribed Edna? Why had he threatened to shoot the boys? Why had he acted so mean about poor Blackberry? It was all such a puzzle that Judy's head seemed to be going round and round and round.

Out of the confusion of her thoughts after she had been locked in the hut, one thing seemed clear—that she must dig out the dam. Now her only logical conclusion was that she must put it back again. And she must do it before the next rain.

Arthur kept well behind the figure on the bicycle. Suddenly he shot the car ahead and all of them turned quickly, straining their eyes to see the shadow man's face. But, to their astonishment, he had dropped completely out of sight.

"Well! I'll be darned!" Arthur exclaimed.

"Think you could identify him, Judy, from what we saw of his back?"

"I'm sure I could," she replied. "Anyway, I would know his hands."

"Oh, so you've seen him before?"

"Quite a few times before," she replied.

"But what makes you think he had anything to do with the dam?" Arthur wanted to know.

"Because—because I saw his cloak hanging in that little hut below it and—and because there was a gun in the pocket——"

"But that wouldn't prove anything," Arthur insisted.

"Would this?" She opened her pocketbook and handed him the envelope she had found. It was addressed to Christopher White, Chief Engineer, Rite-Way Construction Company.

He studied it minutely before he answered. "Yes, if we could be sure that this queer-looking man is Christopher White it would prove one thing—that such a man exists. I questioned that signature on the contract. Where did you find this envelope?"

"In the hut," Judy replied.

"And how did you happen to be there?"

"I told you I'd been hunting for clues." She smiled mysteriously.

Horace, in the back seat of the car, had been sitting motionless. The fearful things he had been hearing and seeing simply paralyzed his powers of speech. How could Judy be so calm, he wondered.

If he had suspected the truth about his sister's disappearance what might he not have thought?

CHAPTER XVI

JUST before she climbed out of the car Judy exacted a promise from the two boys—a promise that they would be back in Dry Brook Hollow again the very next afternoon.

"Dad will be home then," she said, "and he can advise us, but I have a plan I want you to help me carry out. Incidentally, we may find out where that road goes. Better come in your old clothes prepared for hard work."

"Can't you tell us why?" Arthur asked.

She shook her head. "I'd rather not. But you have my word of honor that I will do everything I can—everything——"

"Let her be mysterious," Lois told her brother. "I'd like to come too, may I?" Her dark eyes were bright with excitement and Judy felt as if she had found, in these three young people from Farringdon, fellow lovers of adventure. The fact that they had promised to come all the way to Dry Brook Hollow for an unknown reason, proved it conclusively. "What *are* you going to do tomorrow?" Horace asked as soon as the car was gone.

"I'd like to tell you," his sister replied, "but Arthur and I scared you nearly out of your wits as it is. I'm afraid we will have to leave you out of our Sunday afternoon adventure."

"Aw, Judy."

"But Horace," she protested. "I know you too well. I just wish you could have seen yourself sitting there in the back of Arthur's car with your mouth hanging open. Still," she added hopefully, "there are things that might make me change my mind."

Mrs. Smeed had waited up for them and sat nodding in her chair. She had intended to scold them both but when Judy placed the prize in her lap she forgot her intentions and simply stared.

"I had no idea you could spell like that," she exclaimed when she found her voice. "Were you dancing all this time?"

"Was she?" exclaimed Horace. "Gee, Grandma! I wish you could have seen the fellows all trying to get a dance with her. I enjoyed myself just watching, rather like being brother to a princess, you know, and you should have heard everybody clapping and stamping their feet when she won the prize.''

''Horace,'' asked his sister as they started up the stairs, ''why don't you make me that proud of you sometime?''

''Maybe I will,'' he replied with a sudden light in his eyes.

Judy's only answer was a queer little gulp. She wished desperately that he had the courage to live up to what he must be thinking. If only she could depend on him to help her they might work out a real solution of the gigantic problem that confronted them.

Later, after she had fallen into a fitful sleep, what hope she had for his reformation was smothered by a voice that penetrated the walls with a frightening shriek.

''The dam! The dam! Oh! Oh! Oh!''

She rapped on the wall and called out for him to be quiet. When his wails increased it angered her so much that she got up out of bed to storm at him.

''Might as well have ghosts in the house,'' she fumed, ''as somebody yelling about dams all night. Grandma might hear it and think you were swearing. What have you got to worry about anyway, three miles above the dam?

Sister Bolton is safe enough as long as we're here in Dry Brook Hollow. It's the people in Roulsville that ought to be worrying, but they're not, because they aren't cowards like you. Arthur has a right to worry too," she added as an afterthought, "because he's an engineer and likes to see things done right, but you, you! Oh, I'm so ashamed of you!"

Horace felt ashamed of himself too. Why couldn't he get that dam off his mind? After Judy had gone back to her own room he tossed about restlessly. "The people would all be killed. Nothing short of a miracle could save them." These words Arthur had spoken kept pounding, pounding in his tired brain. He tried to go back to sleep but sleep did not come until nearly morning. Then he slept so heavily Mrs. Smeed had difficulty in awakening him.

"Horace! Horace!" she called. "It's nearly nine o'clock. You'll be late for church."

Horace closed his eyes and turned his face toward the wall. "I'm not going to church," he answered. "Let me sleep."

"Not going to church! Why, Horace! I thought you were supposed to report the sermon. What's the matter? Are you sick?"

"No, just tired. Leave me be."

Mrs. Smeed hurried downstairs to the kitchen where Judy was busily turning pancakes and eating them as fast as they were off the griddle.

"Shall I make some for Horace?" she asked as she stirred the batter.

"Horace—is—sick. He's not going to church." Anxiety was written in every line of her grandmother's face.

"I don't believe it," declared the girl. "I'll go up and see for myself."

"No, no," entreated her grandmother. "Don't—not like you did last night——"

But Judy was already halfway up the stairs.

"Well Sister," she challenged, as soon as she was inside Horace's door, "so you're not going to church because you're afraid of that silly old dam. I might have known it, and grandma is worried to death because she thinks you're sick. Horace, how *can* you be such a coward? Get up and *act* like a man even if you can't *be* one. Doesn't your job on the paper mean anything to you?"

"Aw, leave me be. That sermon isn't so important and you know it. I haven't had a good night's sleep."

"Well, I didn't tell you to scream all night,

did I? Get up!" Judy's voice was more
severe than she realized. The strain of a sleepless night had told on her nerves too but she
had shown no inclination to stay in bed and
rest up in the morning. Instead, she had been
up early writing frantically at the table for a
moment and then glancing over her shoulder
as if she feared someone was watching her. It
was because she had counted on Horace to deliver the note she had been writing that his
refusal to go to church irritated her.

"Aw, Judy," drawled Horace, "leave me
alone."

"Don't 'aw, Judy' me again," she snapped.
"Dad will be home this afternoon and he won't
stand for your being babied. I'll tell him how
you got scared and pretended to be sick. He'll
diagnose your case quick enough. Plain
cowardice! That's all it is."

"But I tell you I don't want to go to church.
Grandpa's got Fanny and I'm too tired to
walk."

"You don't have to walk," retorted Judy
hotly. "Why don't you ride the colt? Grandpa
left him on purpose because he didn't think
you'd want to ride to church on an old work
horse."

"Grandpa knows I never rode the colt,"
Horace protested weakly.

"He knows I did," Judy came back at him.
"I guess if he didn't break my neck he won't
break yours. And I thought you were going to
make me proud of you! You wanted to be let
in on our plan this afternoon. There would be
a chance to show some real courage. We—we
might even prevent this flood—at least until
the people have been warned. But you're
afraid! You'd rather sit by and let other
people get killed while you're all snug and cosy
in your bed."

"You believed what Arthur said then?"
gasped Horace, sitting up.

"I not only believe it," Judy declared, her
voice tense with pent-up anxiety. "I know it's
true. But we still have a little time before it
rains again."

"But what can we do?"

Horace had pulled the covers over his trembling form. Even his lips were pale. Such
outward evidences of his chicken-heartedness
convinced his sister that it would be useless to
confide her plans in him.

"I'm afraid *you* can't do anything," she said
with a curl of her lip. "You aren't even man

enough to ride the colt. If you did something—
anything—to prove to me that you weren't
afraid I might invite you to this—this queer
rescue party of mine at the head of Dry Brook.
Horace, I dare you! I dare you to ride the
colt!"

After Judy had left the room her brother
turned over in his mind the things she had said
and wondered if he ever had been truly courageous. Would it be courageous to go to church
when, in the words of Arthur, he was "taking
his life in his own hands?" Life was very dear
to Horace Bolton.

He came down to breakfast too late to find
any hot pancakes. Mrs. Smeed was busy and
Judy wouldn't make them for him until he
promised to go to church.

The kitchen clock ticked minutes away
regularly, and every minute was that much
nearer church time.

Judy called from outside. "Hurry, Horace!
I have the colt ready, saddle and all. Here,
I'll pull up next to the porch so you can mount
him from there."

"I told you I'm not going," he answered
sullenly.

"Please do," she implored. "I have a letter

for you to give to Peter Dobbs. It's awfully important. You can help me more than you know by just being my messenger."

"Well," conceded Horace at last, "I'll just mount the colt to see how it feels. You know, I never rode any horse but Fanny."

"And she's nothing but an old plug," Judy added, trying to appear casual as her brother put a cautious foot in one stirrup and then swung himself into the saddle. "Isn't his back nice and narrow?"

"Why yes," admitted Horace with some surprise. "He's easier to ride than I thought. Funny how still he stands while we talk. Maybe he isn't as frisky as I supposed he was."

"You'd be surprised," said Judy with a meaning smile. Her wheedling and flattering seemed to be accomplishing what she wanted where teasing and pestering had failed.

"Doesn't the colt have a name?" asked Horace after a pause.

"You can name him after you get home from church. I meant to call him Ginger but maybe he hasn't enough pep for that. Just look at him, the way he stands."

Judy was deliberately deceiving her brother, a thing she did not often do. She had tried teasing, wheedling, flattering, deceit, not merely because she wanted him to deliver her note. Her motive was deeper than that. She wanted to be proud of Horace as Lois was proud of Arthur. For his own good she wanted him to be brave and face these things that scared him so. Down in her heart, Judy had a very real affection for her brother.

"If you see Mrs. Dobbs, give her my love and be sure to give Peter the note. If anything happens so you can't deliver it," Judy added gravely, "open it yourself and do what you can to help me."

"You want me to open your letter to Peter?" Horace questioned doubtfully.

"Yes, if you can't deliver it. It—it will be quite a surprise. But don't drop it. Don't let anybody else get hold of it." She paused. It was after ten-thirty and he ought to be there by eleven. "Just cluck to the colt if you want him to start—or shall I do it?"

Still Horace sat motionless.

"Silence is consent," she said, and signalled the colt to start. "Goodbye, Horace! Grandma! Come out and wave goodbye. Horace is going to church."

Judy had her way.

CHAPTER XVII

HORACE had given in to Judy somewhat against his will. It took some courage even to be a coward, although the frightened boy wasn't thinking exactly that as he bumped along toward Roulsville. On the new cement road the colt quickened his pace, carrying his new master swiftly, swiftly toward the dam.

"Whoa, Ginger!" shouted Horace. It had not taken him long to decide that the name his sister had chosen did fit the colt. Ginger eased into a steady trot and for perhaps five minutes Horace rode comfortably, but the new highway was an invitation to Sunday automobilists and when the first car whizzed by, the colt was off again at a gallop. The second car came too close and he reared on his hind legs and almost threw his rider. Judy hadn't said anything about the colt being afraid of cars so Horace supposed the fault must lay in the way he handled him. He pulled hard on the reins, but instead of slowing down, Ginger

whirled in a dizzy circle and darted off faster
than ever with Horace bouncing up and down
on his back like a rubber ball.

Church bells in Roulsville began to ring just
as Horace passed the giant dam. The colt
paused, listened, sniffed the air and whinnied
to the other horses who were grazing in the
pasture below the dam.

The cracks in the dam yawned wide. Below,
the hut where the workmen had kept their tools
was surrounded by water on three sides and a
plank had been placed across the pool by the
door. It puzzled Horace to see a thin column
of smoke issuing from behind the hut. Then a
hand appeared and flipped a cigarette into the
surrounding swamp. Horace had not noticed
this swamp before and wondered whether or
not it was there when they had watched the dam
by moonlight. Probably it was, but he felt sure
the black cracks had widened. Deliberately,
he turned his face away from the sight that so
terrified him and rode on toward Roulsville.

The ten-fifty whistled away down the track
and Horace realized that he had made the whole
distance to town in less than fifteen minutes.
Old Fanny took more than twice that long.

The colt reared again at the sound of the

train and dashed across the track. Horace just
managed to turn him into quiet River Street
at the end of which was their home, with the
church directly across from it. Bells were still
chiming and again the colt paused to listen.
They seemed to have a soothing effect on his
wild spirits and he trotted along obediently
until Horace stopped him at the church steps.
He hitched him to a telephone pole and, with
a sigh of relief, entered the half empty church.
Strange that it should still be early, but time
had not kept pace with Ginger.

Feeling a little sick from so much bumping,
he slumped into a back seat and, through half-
closed eyes, watched the people filing in to their
places. Mr. and Mrs. Dobbs were there as
usual but Peter was not with them. Most of
the other faces were familiar. Horace was surprised to see Lois, Lorraine, Donald and
Arthur enter through a side door. The girls
were dressed almost alike in light colored suits
with close fitting hats to match. He remembered what Judy had told them about wearing
old clothes and wondered if they had brought
them in the car. Did they intend coming home
with him after church and if not what could
these four young people from Farringdon be

doing in Roulsville on a Sunday morning?
They smiled and nodded to him and took a seat
right across the aisle. Horace could hear Lorraine's sweet voice above the others when they
rose to sing.

The services were beautiful and strangely
appropriate. If the minister had prepared his
sermon especially for Horace it could not have
been more to the point. He even read a pas-
sage from the Bible telling how Jesus rode a
colt "whereon never man sat." Courage and
strength were the virtues he emphasized
throughout his entire sermon.

"Life is a battle, here and now," he said.
"Without courage we cannot succeed in anything, for the very things we fear will become
our masters. So we must get into the struggle,
square our shoulders and fight—to win."

In this Roulsville church it was the custom
to pass the collection plate after the sermon
instead of before. While the organ played and
coins rattled, Horace sat as if in a trance. The
sermon he had heard confirmed what Judy had
told him many, many times. He had not been
strong; he had not been courageous; his fears,
in truth, had mastered him. Suddenly he sat
up straight and braced his shoulders, not real-

izing that the minister and all the rest of the congregation had their heads bowed in prayer. Horace was never to forget that Sunday.

After the services Mr. Dobbs and his wife spoke to him and he asked about Peter.

"Oh, the boy's gone for all day," Mrs. Dobbs said with pride in her voice. "It's some legal case he's working on, just for practice."

"I see." Horace fingered the note in his pocket. If it was really important perhaps he ought to read it as Judy had told him. He was burning with a desire to do something—anything—to prove to his sister that he was not a coward. Riding the colt was something, but it was not enough.

Lois, Lorraine, Donald and Arthur had left through the side door, but met Horace on the church steps just as he was loosening Ginger's bridle.

"So this is the colt!" exclaimed Lois. "Judy told me about riding him to town when she sold her berries."

"He *is* a beauty," praised Lorraine. "A perfect saddle horse. I should not mind riding him myself. Do you ride him much, Horace?"

"This is the first time, but it won't be the

last," the boy added resolutely. "How does it happen that you are in Roulsville so early?"

"Arthur will tell you about that," replied Lois. "He's the funniest boy. Just because he believes the dam is dangerous he can't keep away from it. Now that the new road is open all the way through I suppose we'll see more of the dam than ever."

"That's right," declared Arthur with a smile. "I guess it's like war. Dangerous things do attract somehow."

"This colt ought to attract you then," said Horace dryly. "It's all a fellow's life is worth to ride him."

Lois laughed softly. Judy had told her of her experience with the train when they exchanged confidences over their sodas.

"Why don't you drive up to the farm for dinner?" continued Horace, "Grandma always has plenty and Judy expects you afterwards."

"So nice of you to invite us," said Lorraine sweetly, "but we're dining with friends here in Roulsville. Lois and the boys may come up later."

"We'll be looking for you," called Horace as he swung himself over the colt's back and turned the animal toward home.

Then he remembered Judy's note and halted the colt almost in front of the Dobbs' home while he read it. The penciled scrawl was written hastily but the thought behind it was clear and well expressed.

"I promised not to talk," Judy had written, "but I never promised not to write." Then followed the whole story of her abduction and imprisonment and her strange promise told as concisely as though it had been prepared for the press. At the end of the letter she asked for Peter's help in rebuilding the small dam at the head of Dry Brook.

"Donald and Arthur will help too," the letter continued, "and Horace may be of some use. The work *must* be done before the next hard rain. The fact that bribes are being offered proves that Charlie Austin as well as the shadow man and those two workmen know that the dam may break at any moment. We've got to do something about it. You can help me better than any one else because you won't be afraid. Judy."

It took several minutes after he had finished reading the note for its full import to impress itself on Horace's mind.

His sister kidnaped! Alone in that dreary

hut all night! He remembered the mark on her
face when they had found her in the morning.
To think it had been done by that horrible looking man they had overtaken on the road. If he
was a man—"Ugh!" Horace shuddered at the
very thought of that skull-like head. But Judy
had made her strange promise not because she
was afraid, but because she wanted to be free
to help.

"Oh, Judy! Judy!" he said under his
breath. "If I could only be worthy of a sister
like you."

The letter was a challenge, clear and unmis-
takable. An opportunity to answer it came to
Horace while he still held it in his hand. He
had forgotten momentarily that the dam, a
great white giant ready to let loose its fury,
crouched in the valley above him. The slip of
paper had so absorbed him that he had not
noticed the strange hush that had settled over
the little town.

Suddenly things took on unusual colors, some
appearing yellow, others purple, blue-gray or
green. People began to walk a little more
swiftly and animals paused and sniffed the air.
Ginger whinnied and his call sounded as if he
were warning some one of something.

Horace could not understand it until he looked up and saw the sky. Actually it was yellow. Great bluish clouds that looked more like smoke or some deadly vapor, billowed out of the west. Those fears which he had determined to conquer rushed back with renewed force. Everything else paled into insignificance. This was the storm that Arthur had predicted. The heavy air seemed to be closing in upon Roulsville, stifling it. Disaster was written in that yellow sky.

The frightened boy tried to calm himself by observing how peaceful everything was. Hardly a leaf stirred on the shade trees that lined the quiet streets. Roulsville was only a small town with the paper mill its one big industry and most of the inhabitants were plain working men with modest little homes. He could see the industrious housewives hurrying to close their windows before the storm broke. The Dobbs' cat, mother of the lost Blackberry, waited, stretched on the doormat, for her owners to return from church. Probably they were still grouped around the vestibule talking. Nobody seemed to be in a hurry, not even the colt.

Across this peaceful picture flashed a sudden

streak of lightning followed by a low rumble
of thunder and rain coming down Dry Brook
Hollow like a sheet. Horace could see the ad-
vancing rainstorm before he felt it. Like a
thing of life it marched rapidly down the
valley.

Other people opened umbrellas, closed windows and doors, did all the little practical
things that people do when it rains, not realizing, as Horace did, that this thing which was
descending upon Roulsville was no ordinary
storm. Blue-gray clouds had covered the yellow sky and a weird whistling sounded through
the gathering darkness. Ginger braced his body
against the wind and refused to budge while
his master clung to the reins, too frightened to
think coherently. Rain beat against his face,
cutting, blinding.

Still Horace did not try to hurry the colt.
Somewhere in the back of his mind an idea that
he must be courageous kept him from obviously
running away although he felt certain that this
ride might be a race with the flood. The lonely
road up Dry Brook Hollow was blanketed in
water. Ginger shook his dripping mane and
began a steady slow trot for home.

A dazzling flash of lightning revealed houses,

trees and tall smoke stacks in black outline. Another flash so close that it looked like fire! Then came a third flash followed by a crash, a roar and a long, loud rumbling that sounded like something being torn apart and the rushing of water. Panic seized Horace and he began to scream.

"It's the dam! The dam! The dam is breaking!"

Ginger snorted. He reared and circled, then darted off like a flash in the opposite direction —back to Roulsville!

Down through Main Street raced the boy on the colt, screaming, screaming. People surged out of every building and in an instant all had caught up the cry.

"The dam is breaking! The dam is breaking! Run for the hills!"

Automobile horns honked and somebody rang the fire bell. Somebody else rang the church bell and together they made a wild discord. The wet streets had become a seething mass of terror-stricken humanity swarming in two directions.

On one side of the valley were a few dwelling houses built on stilts along a street called Hill Street. On the other side was the park with steep gravel roads winding in and out. Automobiles raced to both these high spots, filled to capacity. Cars stalled and their frantic occupants abandoned them and left them blocking the way of others who would climb to safety.

But Horace did not turn Ginger toward the park or toward Hill Street. His duty was clearly to warn every living person in Roulsville before he saved himself. That was the challenge in Judy's letter and this time he would not fail her.

On he raced straight through Main Street and turned down River Street where belated churchgoers were still talking in the shelter of the vestibule. Horace called out to them and took one last look at the empty gray house across the street, the house that had been his home. The fire bell kept on ringing and more church bells joined in the warning until the din almost drowned out the noise of the storm.

Arthur and Donald appeared from somewhere and between them they carried Lorraine who had fainted. They piled her on Lois' lap in their big blue car which already held more than a dozen people. They saw Horace and called out to him.

"Save yourself! Save yourself! Can't you hear the bells? Follow us to the pavilion."

The last words trailed away as the Bluebird rolled out of sight. But Horace did not follow.

"I'm being brave," he thought to himself. "This time I'm not going to run away from danger."

The sky was sending down torrents of rain. It splashed about the horse's knees for the street had become filled with water. It dripped off his body and glistened on his back. Lightning zig-zagged across the sky and a second and third crash sounded almost as loud as the first one. The blinding rain did not permit any one, either Horace or the people on the hillsides, to see up the valley as far as the dam. Thunder and lightning raged and each new crash struck terror to his heart. But he remembered his grandfather working with Sam Tucker on a farm a mile farther down, and kept on. Mrs. Smeed had said the Lord would punish him for working on Sunday. But he deserved no such punishment as this.

The fire bell must have sounded a long way for when Horace reached it, Sam Tucker's field was deserted. Grandfather Smeed was probably safe in the farmhouse on the hillside.

Again the thunder roared and in his mind Horace compared it with the sound that had set him screaming. Another roar and a loud rumbling that sounded like the rushing of water.

"Here comes the flood!" he cried hoarsely. "Gee there, Ginger. Giddap!"

CHAPTER XVIII

ALL JUDY'S FAULT

WHEN Horace first galloped out of sight down the road Judy had felt triumphant. Mrs. Smeed hastened out on the porch just in time to see the colt quicken his pace as they turned on to the cement.

"You shouldn't have done it, Judy," she said reproachfully. "That colt's going for all that's in him and the poor boy acted sick."

"Scared sick," sniffed Judy. "That was all that was the matter with him. I coaxed and teased him until I finally got him to go. If he comes back acting a little more like a man, you'll have me to thank for it."

"And," wailed Mrs. Sneed, "if he comes back with a broken leg, I'll have you to thank for *that* too."

"Yes, whatever happens, it's all my fault. But I'm not worrying."

Nevertheless, Judy sat there on the porch steps for an hour, holding a book and doing nothing else but worry. She remembered that

the ten-fifty was due in Roulsville just about
the time Horace would be crossing the track.
If she could not make the colt stop when the
train was coming, how could he? She worried
when she thought of the note he carried in his
pocket. Suppose the shadow overtook him, suspected, read what Judy had written. Her
brother might disappear as completely as had
her kitten. Again Judy dismissed this thought
as being too unreasonable.

A great many cars were trying out the new
road that Sunday. She could see them clearly
through the trees. One was a big blue car
that looked like Arthur's. The driver looked
like Arthur too, and the two pretty girls in
the car were Lois and Lorraine. Donald
Carter was there too. But they weren't stopping. Judy hoped that they had not forgotten
their promise to come in the afternoon. She
knew it would be utterly impossible for her to
rebuild the dam alone and there was so little
time. She wondered how Peter made out with
the note. Was it, she asked herself, breaking
her promise to write what she had pledged herself not to speak?

"Maybe I shouldn't have asked Horace to
read it," she thought anxiously. "He can't do

anything about it and it will simply scare him out of his senses.''

Presently Mrs. Smeed came out on the porch again to sit beside her granddaughter. She brought a tie that she was knitting for Horace and soon the click of her needles kept time with the kitchen clock's noisy ticking. The clock struck eleven and paused after each dong.

"Services will be starting now," commented Mrs. Smeed.

Judy knew what her grandmother was thinking but, fortunately, her own unhappy thoughts were known only to herself.

"Some one must help before it's too late!" she reflected desperately.

This waiting and waiting for people to come was almost unbearable. But how good it would seem to have her parents home again. The distracted girl felt as if she needed her father's understanding sympathy and her mother's tender advice more than ever. Mrs. Smeed, who only unbent on rare occasions, was so unlike Judy's mother who seemed young, even to her daughter. The yearly trip that she and the doctor took back to the quiet summer resort where they spent their honeymoon proved that both of them were young at heart.

"Mother and Dad are probably having the time of their lives," Judy remarked thoughtfully. "But it will be such a comfort to have them home."

"Small comfort to me if Horace gets hurt," answered her grandmother shortly.

For several minutes Judy did not attempt any further conversation. Still the clock ticked; still the knitting needles clicked. Everything else was too quiet, except now and then when a car went by on the road. They could be heard distinctly although Judy never remembered being able to hear them before. The air was so still not a leaf moved. The sky —Judy simply hadn't thought about the sky. When she did think it was with a panicky suddenness. Skies weren't ordinarily yellow except at sunset.

Mrs. Smeed put down her knitting. "Judy," she said, "will you look at that sky?"

"I am looking," she replied faintly. "Does that mean a storm?"

"It means a cloud-burst if I know anything about weather. Just look at those smoky clouds."

The girl on the steps did not answer for fear of betraying her thoughts.

She had told Horace that the colt was safe. And yet, if a storm came, her brother might be riding to his death. She had told her grandparents she picked blackberries all day that awful day when she had set Dry Brook free.

What lies they all were and how she hated herself for telling them! It seemed impossible for her to sit calmly on the steps and think such thoughts without her grandmother knowing. Gathering some books in her arms, she started toward the barn where she could be alone.

Before she had gone two steps, a loud peal of thunder, lightning, rain and her grandmother's frightened cry arrested her.

"I won't go away now," she said. "I know you're afraid of thunder."

"It isn't that. Judy, you know it isn't that. It's Horace and the colt in this. Oh, Judy!" Mrs. Smeed pressed her head against the wet porch rail and began to moan.

"Don't take on so," coaxed her granddaughter. "You make me feel like a criminal. How did I know it was going to rain?"

"Of course you didn't, but it was your fault he went and I'm sure the poor boy was sick. Go in and see what time it is."

"Twelve-thirty," announced Judy in a shaky voice as she studied the kitchen clock. "Church lets out at twelve-thirty. He may wait till after the rain."

This information consoled Mrs. Smeed, but not her granddaughter. Judy knew about the dam and if even a little storm might cause the disaster, what of a deluge like this? Secretly she hoped Horace would brave the storm and that the colt would let loose all the energy in his body and gallop his hardest for home.

The muddy waters of Dry Brook raced along in a swift torrent, higher and higher. It was too late even to attempt to control them. Judy's only hope lay in the possibility that Arthur had been wrong. "Five years or five minutes," he had said. It could be five years, but would it be? *Would* it be?

Rain had driven the girl and her grandmother inside where they still watched the storm from the kitchen window. Neither of them thought of preparing dinner, although Judy's parents were expected at one o'clock. She had been happy in anticipating their return home. Now there might not be any home! She stared at the road with anxious eyes and suddenly a car shot past.

"It's Mother and Dad!" she shrieked, "and they're not stopping! They're going to Roulsville!"

"Maybe they'll meet Horace and come back with him."

"Oh, Grandma! I hope they do. If anything happens——"

Mrs. Smeed saw her anxious face and frowned. "Thought you weren't going to worry."

Her granddaughter did not answer. She had pressed her hot forehead against the windowpane, still staring, half in anticipation, half in dread. More cars went by in a dizzy procession. All of them, it seemed, were going toward Roulsville. No! Not all. One had streaked by, headed for Farringdon. It was Charlie Austin's yellow roadster.

Judy caught at her throat and started back from the window as an alarming thought flashed across her mind. He was getting away! Charlie Austin knew there was danger and was getting away before any of the blame could be placed on him.

"I'll fix him," she said fiercely. Without stopping to reason any further she ran to the telephone and put in a long distance call to

"IT'S THE DAM! THE DAM! THE DAM IS BREAKING!"

The Vanishing Shadow.   *Page 157*

Farringdon. Her grandmother, struck speechless, could only watch and listen.

"Police Department," Judy's voice gritted
over the wire. "Hello. Yes, I wanted the police station. Stop Charlie Austin in a yellow
roadster——"

The sentence was never finished. Judy
dropped the receiver as though it had been
charged with a deadly current. She started
back from the telephone with a scream as a
mighty roar shook the house. Every piece of
furniture in it trembled as with the force of an
explosion.

Forgetting caution, she cried out in distress,
"The dam! The dam! Oh! It must be the
dam. It's breaking and everybody will be
killed!"

But Mrs. Smeed made no answer. She had
slumped down in her chair unconscious, and,
for a moment, Judy thought her grandmother
was dead. Afterwards she wondered how she
had acted so sanely in the face of such a
tragedy. Automatically her feet moved toward
the kitchen. She poured out a pitcher of cold
water and mopped her forehead until at last
Mrs. Smeed opened her eyes.

"Oh, Grandma!" she cried, suddenly embracing her. "Thank God we've got each other. For a minute I thought I had been left—all—alone."

A weird noise sounded down Dry Brook Hollow, the screeching of ambulances, the roar of fire engines and the rumble of a continual procession of speeding cars. There could be no doubt in the mind of either the girl or her grandmother. It had been the dam and those ambulances were racing to the scene of disaster, perhaps too late.

Judy wrung her hands in anguish and her eyes burned with tears that would not come. If Horace had been killed it was all her fault! Her Dad and Mother too, racing on toward Roulsville! Nothing short of a miracle could save them. Mr. and Mrs. Dobbs and Peter would be killed, their beautiful home washed away. Arthur! Donald! Lois! Lorraine! Her patient old grandfather, all of them! All of them! And it was her fault. Everything was her fault.

"Child! Can't you do anything but stand and stare?" Mrs. Smeed's strained voice sounded a long way off.

"What else can I do? Oh, what else *can* I do? It's like the end of the world."

"It *is* the end of the world," groaned Mrs. Smeed. "It's the judgment of the Lord."

"No, no, not that! Just a judgment upon me. And if Horace is alive I'll never, never tease him again. I'll do everything to make him happy. Oh, I knew it would happen! Grandma, he told us. Arthur told us. Charlie Austin and the workmen knew it too—and that awful shadow man. The real reason Horace wouldn't go to church was because he felt afraid of that dam. But I made him go. Oh, if he's killed I'll never forgive myself. If Dad and Mother are killed I want to die too!"

But as the clock ticked away minute after minute Judy grew more certain that they would never come home.

"I can't stand this waiting another second," she cried at length. "I'm going to get them."

"How, child? How?" wailed her grandmother.

"Well, at least I can—I can—see to things—if the worst has happened."

"Go then! Better take your warm coat. You may need it. Now get me that spirits of ammonia bottle up in the medicine closet and I'll manage somehow. Find out about as many folks as you can. Judy! You haven't had a bite to eat. You can't go three miles on an empty stomach.''

"I couldn't eat," cried Judy. "Food would choke me. Here's your ammonia, Grandma, so you won't faint. I'm going now. Goodbye!"

CHAPTER XIX

IT NEVER occurred to Judy to hail one of the speeding cars and none stopped to offer her a ride. Ahead of her stretched miles and miles of white road and Roulsville seemed and endless distance away as she dodged this way and that to avoid the maddening stream of cars. Wherever they all came from she did not know, but she perceived that they were going in both directions. An ambulance passed, going toward Dry Brook Hollow. Judy bit her lip, turned her face away and hurried on.

After what seemed ages, she finally came in sight of the dam and looked. She looked again and then stared in terrified fascination. Only a shallow muddy pool remained where a great lake of clear water once had sparkled. The concrete dam that she had once loved for its beauty lay in three broken pieces, sprawled across the wreckage that had been the paper mill. Below, though she could not see that far, must be her home—flattened out like that paper mill. Her parents in their car! The church where Horace went! Sam Tucker's hay field— where her grandfather had been working! Judy tried not to think. She tried ever so hard not to think but she couldn't help thinking of the terrible thing that had surely happened.

The hut in which Judy had been imprisoned was gone without a trace. Could it be crushed and buried beneath the middle section of the broken dam or could it simply have vanished with its ghostly occupant inside?

But Judy was too heart-sick and miserable to ponder any question except the all-important one—what had happened to Horace and her parents?

As she came in sight of the first few houses in Roulsville she relinquished what little hope she had for their safety. A noise like the distant humming of bees came to her ears but at first the distracted girl did not realize that it was the sound of people's voices. Instead of looking toward the hillside she glanced furtively behind her, half expecting to see the shadow. Then, as she turned, her gaze rested upon something that actually terrified her.

The hut was planted in the road ahead of her, almost blocking it. It was not crushed or tipped over as the other houses were, but stood as if it had been built there. A startled cry escaped from Judy's lips as she beheld something moving on the roof of the hut. Was it a shadow? No, it seemed to have body and substance. It crawled!

Judy knew that her eyes were dim with tears, that none of these things she had been seeing were distinct, that her mind was as clouded as her vision. Even so, what could a moving black shadow be doing on the roof of her prison unless it were crouching, ready to spring—to grasp her by the throat with its long, chalk-white hands?

Suddenly she felt weak, cowardly. She wanted to run away—anywhere—just so that she need not pass that hut. It was then that she turned up a muddy side street and caught sight of the crowd on the hillside.

Some of them were sitting in their parked cars. Others stood around in groups, talking, or rested on benches in the little park. But most of them were crowded into the pavilion, the same pavilion that Judy had last seen gay with streamers of blue and yellow. These people were talking too and, if Judy's ears were playing her no tricks, actually laughing.

She rushed headlong toward the pavilion and elbowed her way through the crowd until she found someone that she knew. That someone happened to be Mr. Dobbs.

"Well! Well!" he exclaimed, turning to his wife who stood beside him, "if it isn't Judy Bolton, sister of our hero."

Judy stared at him. Had Horace done something so ridiculous that Mr. Dobbs was making fun of him?

"Maybe she doesn't know," Mrs. Dobbs ventured, touching his arm.

"Sure she knows. Everybody knows. All they're waiting for is to get a glimpse of him. Those photographers and newspaper men, for instance——"

"But I don't know, Mr. Dobbs," Judy broke in. "I haven't the slightest idea what you are talking about. I—I expected to find you—all—dead. However did you escape?"

"How we escaped is still a mystery," he replied. "That brother of yours raced through town on the colt and warned us. He must have had a premonition. At any rate we had plenty of time to reach the hills safely. Why, we actually watched the dam break. And I reckon just about everybody in town is saved."

"Really?" It was incredible. The miracle had happened and, in some strange way, Horace was responsible. "You mean to say it was my brother—my brother—a hero. Are you sure the boy who warned the people was Horace?"

Mr. Dobbs assured her again that it was no one else. "And if you thought you galloped the colt you should have seen him! And shouting himself hoarse in the bargain! Talk about Paul Revere's ride! And the deuce of it all is, how did he know the dam was going to break?"

Judy shook her head. "Where is he now?" she asked. "We might find out from him."

"He'll turn up soon," Mr. Dobbs began, but she detected the anxious note in his voice.

"Is he—missing?" she demanded.

"Maybe across the valley," the old man replied vaguely. "See, there's quite a crowd over there."

"I see. But where are Mother and Dad?"

"Were they in town too?" Mrs. Dobbs asked in great concern. "I haven't seen them but perhaps they are over on Hill Street with Horace. Your father would surely be helping people who were injured or were suffering from shock. I wouldn't worry, Judy dear.

They'll come across the valley as soon as the débris is cleared away and the streets drained so they can. Peter is down there helping the men now."

"I wish I could help," Judy cried. "It will be awful waiting and not knowing."

"You might carry a pail of coffee down to them," Mrs. Dobbs suggested. "They're dispensing food and coffee from that truck. See, over there where the crowd is."

Looking in the direction that Mrs. Dobbs indicated, Judy saw women and children crowding around, drinking eagerly from paper cups or milk bottles. They clung to each other, glad to be alive.

Then one of the girls who was serving them turned around and Judy recognized her.

"Why, it's Lois," she exclaimed, "and Lorraine is with her."

"Just so," replied Mrs. Dobbs. "Their fathers donated the food. They have been here working like little queen bees ever since the dam broke."

As soon as they saw her, they rushed forward, the same question on the lips of both of them, "Is Horace safe?"

Judy could only shake her head and, in turn,

ask about her father. The girls had heard
nothing of him but one old woman, a patient of
the doctor's, said she thought she recognized his
car across the valley. It was quite a distance
away and none of them could be sure.

"Was anybody killed?" Judy asked her anxiously.

"Only one," she replied. "The president of
the paper mill. He started to go back when he
saw that the dam hadn't broken. We all warned
him. 'That boy seems to know what he's talking about' we all said, but he wouldn't listen
to us."

"He's Mr. Rubin, the one Arthur wanted to
see," Lois put in. "Remember?"

"How could I forget?" Judy exclaimed.
"We never dreamed that the next time we came
to the pavilion it would be—like this?"

"We can be thankful we are all alive," the
woman reminded her.

"We may not be," Judy said gravely. She
had no assurance that any of her own family
were safe—except her grandmother and even
she was apt to faint again—there in the house
alone.

"Sure and he's safe," another neighbor declared. "The streets were empty when the dam

broke—and so were all the houses. Judy, that brother—I guess we'd forgotten. He's grown up quite some—straight as a soldier. Lands! How we all scattered when we heard him yelling about the dam."

"I'm sorry I called him 'Sister,' " Lorraine ventured in her most humble tone. And Lois added, "Judy, aren't you proud of Horace?"

"Proud of him!" she exclaimed. "Why, I'm bursting with pride—b-but he's—he's missing." Her eyes were misty. She could hardly see to steady the pail while Lois filled it with coffee. "Didn't anybody see him turn for the hills?"

A man stepped up and vounteered a final bit of information. "The last we seen of 'im, Miss, 'e was 'eadin' straight down the valley toward Sam Tucker's farm."

"He may have gone to warn Grandpa. But would he have had time? What time was it—then—when you saw him?"

"Mebbe five minutes 'fore the dam busted. We barely had time to reach the hills ourselves. But that there colt was goin' like mad. Reckon 'e's safe, Miss. After savin' all the rest of us 't ain't likely 'e'd let hisself get drownded. Now, is it?"

Judy spilled a little of the coffee. It was hot
and burned her foot. But she paid no attention
to that. She must find Horace and perhaps
Peter could help her. She ran all the way to
the valley where she had been told the boys
were working.

Quite an army of them were there and Judy
recognized Arthur and Donald at once. Lois
had told her they were there. Peter, however,
was not with them.

"He's trying to fix up that hut over there,"
Arthur explained, pointing. "He says there's
a cot inside and his grandparents must have
some place to stay tonight. Their home is in
ruins and even the car was wrecked."

"They can't stay in *that* hut!" Judy cried.
"Pass the coffee around to the boys, Arthur.
And here's a bag of rolls. I'm going now—to
get Peter." The last words of her sentence
were flung over her shoulder as she ran blindly
toward the little house that she had once called
"the pit." She dared not look at the roof for
fear she would see that crawling shadow, lose
heart and be afraid to go inside where Peter
Dobbs was.

He turned suddenly as her form appeared in
the doorway. He had been bending over the

cot, removing the soiled covers. He held one in his hand.

"Judy Bolton!" he exclaimed. "Any news of Horace?"

"Drop that!" she cried in alarm, and Peter let go of the blanket without asking why. "No," she continued gravely, "there's no news, except that a man saw him racing toward Sam Tucker's farm five minutes before the dam broke. I can't believe it—Horace—my brother. Peter, he was always so—so—" Her voice broke and Peter Dobbs strode forward and put a strong arm over her trembling shoulders.

"I know, Judy. We must find him. If we can get through we might hunt down toward the farm."

"And find Grandpa too—and I'm not sure that even Dad and Mother are safe. Someone thought it was their car across the valley. Peter!" Judy stopped short as a scratching sound came from the ceiling of the little hut. "Let's get out of here. There's something on the roof!"

"Someone could stay in that hut," Peter protested as Judy dragged him along.

"You'll stay with us," Judy said in a commanding tone. "Grandma has plenty of room and you *can't* stay in that hut. It's the most awful place in the world. There was a black thing crawling on the roof."

"You must have been dreaming."

"I wasn't. I saw it." She looked back apprehensively at the hut and pointed an eloquent finger toward the roof. "There it is now— something black—waving back and forth like a plume. Oh! I may be silly, but if you read my note you know——"

"Your note?" Peter broke in. "What note?"

"I sent it this morning by Horace. Didn't he—didn't he—deliver it?"

"I haven't seen him," Peter replied. "I followed the crowd to the hillside after I made sure Grandma and Grandpa were safe. Everybody was talking about Horace's bravery and that's how I heard."

Judy was still staring at the roof of the hut.

"It's gone!" she exclaimed.

"What's gone?"

"That shadow—on the roof."

Taking her gently by the shoulders, Peter turned her around where she could no longer see the hut. It wasn't like Judy to be frightened by shadows when there were so many grave

problems to be answered. He had not read the
note. He could not know that the distracted
girl believed that the shadow—not the flood—
was responsible for her brother's disappearance. That creature would have pursued him as
it had pursued her when she "knew too much."
Perhaps the shadow man, even now, had possession of the note and was lying in wait for
her. Perhaps he had possession of Horace——

"Peter, for Heaven's sake, say something,"
she burst out. "Anything, but talk as hard as
you can just so I won't need to think any more
until we find Horace."

"All right," he replied, trying to act cheerful. "That black thing you saw was probably
a piece of wreckage that had fallen on the roof
of the hut. A roof has two sides, you know,
and when it disappeared it must have slipped
down on the other side. As you must have observed, the wind is strong. Or perhaps it was
a shadow——"

"Peter! Not about shadows. Don't talk
about shadows."

"Just as you say, my dear," he went on hur-
riedly as they continued down the road.
"Grandma made some blackberry tarts this
morning out of the jam she bought from you.

They were crisp and brown and just oozed delicious blackberries——"

"Peter! Not about blackberries."

He shrugged his shoulders. "My talk doesn't seem to please you. Wouldn't it be more sensible to be honest with ourselves and talk about the thing on both of our minds—finding Horace. In my opinion the most sensible thing to do is get across the valley. If you don't mind wading in water up to your waist we might be able to make it."

"I don't mind anything," Judy cried, "as long as we find him. If Dad's over there he'll help us."

Accordingly they made their way toward the cross street that the boys had been clearing of débris.

"I thought I might be able to get through with the car," Arthur explained. "Another couple of hours and the street will be clear."

"Another couple of hours and it may be too late to get the story into the *Herald's* last edition," spoke up Donald Carter, pausing and wiping his muddy hands on his handkerchief.

Judy had forgotten that there were such things as newspapers. Now she realized that this was about the biggest news that a paper could feature. And Donald Carter was reporting it—Horace's story.

"If you find him," the young reporter continued. "Better plan some method of signalling. Everybody is anxious about him."

"I'll wave my handkerchief," Judy replied. "Once if he's still missing, twice if he's safe and—and three times if—if—he is dead."

CHAPTER XX

PROGRESS was slow along the inundated street. In some places the sidewalk was high and dry. Then, where wreckage blocked the flow of water, Peter and Judy would climb over stacks of loose boards, uprooted trees and bits of household furniture. Once Judy caught sight of a boot that had been washed away and, for one terrified moment, thought that a man might be buried in the wreckage.

They were more than halfway across the valley when Judy stepped off the curb and up to her waist in water.

"It looks even deeper ahead," said Peter, taking a few more experimental steps, "and if the bridge is washed out we couldn't possibly get across the river."

"Maybe we're near enough to call out to someone," Judy suggested. She moved back to the sidewalk again and stood there wet and shivering.

"We'll do that," declared Peter. He cupped

175

his hands and shouted but no one seemed to
hear. Then a man, nearer than the others,
turned his face toward the valley. Peter
shouted again and this time Judy joined him.
The man, who had been one of their near neigh-
bors, came closer. They shouted again.

"Is Horace there?"

They waited breathlessly but the man shook
his head. Judy uttered a low moan, turned and
waved her handkerchief—once. Then she
clutched Peter's coat sleeve as he shouted again.

"Is Dr. Bolton there?"

This time the man nodded. He pointed to the
car that Judy had noticed before and beside it
bent a familiar figure in a gray suit. She
waved frantically, trying to attract his attention but he seemed to be busy over some figure
who lay on the back seat. Judy could not make
out whether it was a man or a woman, only that
the figure was covered with a white sheet.

"It must be a dead person!" she exclaimed
and the agonized look in her eyes told Peter
what she was thinking.

"The man said Horace was not there," he
assured her with a cheerfulness that he did not
feel, "so he must be on our side of the valley,
maybe in the woods below the park."

"But he would have come home——"

She stopped speaking as her eyes rested upon the spot where their home had been. The gray house was there, at least the main part of it. But the porches had been torn off and a piece of the demolished garage had been forced through one of the lower windows. The house had tipped a little too and leaned crazily forward, almost colliding with the ruined church across from it.

Peter's home, too, was sadly demolished. It was some relief to be out of the devastated town and back on the hillside wrapped in her warm coat. Her grandmother had been right about her needing it.

The boys had made considerable progress with their work of clearing away the wreckage and Arthur declared that in another hour the doctor might be able to drive across. He thought there was little possibility of the bridge being washed away as it was built with strong cement, much stronger than the material that had been used to build the broken dam. The prospect of Horace's returning within the hour seemed less likely.

"I suppose it makes a better newspaper story with the hero missing," Judy said bitterly, eyeing Donald whose apparent cheerfulness irritated her.

"It would make a better newspaper story," he returned quietly, "if we organized a searching party and combed those woods. He may be only hurt."

"Thrown from the colt, perhaps," Peter replied, studying Judy's face. Her eyes were fixed on a spot in the woods below the park where something was moving in the brush.

"That's the place our searching party ought to head for," he exclaimed.

"Can't we take a couple of police officers along," Judy ventured in a shaky voice. Those moving bushes suggested more trouble. They reminded her of that awful day in the beech grove when she had darted after the shadow.

A group of policemen stood nearby and three of them joined the young people as they started up the valley.

"Were you looking for my brother too?" Judy asked the uniformed man who strode along ahead of her.

"Not much," he replied gruffly. "My business is to track down criminals. We're after the officials of the construction company that built this dam."

"Christopher White! The engineer!"

"He's the man!" the policeman exclaimed.

"Know anything about him?"

"A little."

"Well, let's have it."

"One of you policemen ought to go back and search that hut," Judy suggested. "Right beside the road. See?"

He nodded.

"I know for sure that your Mr. White spends considerable time in there. In fact you'll find his cloak hanging on a nail in the corner."

"That would identify him, sure!" exclaimed the other officer. "They tell me he's a peculiar fellow. Has a habit of vanishing whenever anybody puts him to task for his mistakes. But he won't vanish this time," he added fiercely as they started back toward the hut.

"It looks as if he had vanished already," Peter remarked dryly.

"Better look on the roof too," Judy called after the retreating policemen. "You may find your missing Mr. White up there."

Only one of the officers remained with them to continue their search. Presently a rustling was heard in the bushes. Judy gave an exclamation, first of surprise and then of dismay.

It was Ginger. But he had come without a rider. His saddle was empty—empty——

Donald Carter offered to take the horse back with him, saying that he really ought to be on the job at the newspaper office. The others explained the identity of the colt to the policeman and the search went on with renewed vigor.

"Here are the tracks," he pointed out. "The horse must have come from the woods this way. We ought to find the boy before long."

Perhaps Peter was right and her brother had only been hurt, Judy thought hopefully as she darted this way and that searching on all sides of the path that the colt had made through the bushes. In some places the officer was obliged to pause and study the ground closely to determine the right direction. On and on they went until they were almost a mile below the park and just opposite Sam Tucker's farm. Judy looked anxiously across the valley where the farmhouse on the hillside was still intact, but she could see where water had flooded the hayfield and washed the grass smooth nearly to the door. The line of smoke rising from the chimney of the house told her that her grandfather was probably inside with the Tucker family, well and safe.

The colt's tracks suddenly turned downhill. They led on toward the valley until they came to the flood-line and just below it a grassy cleared place.

"This way," Arthur beckoned them. "Ah, here is Ginger's bridle. It looks as if he had been tied to this tree and then broken away. Horace must have been here to tie him. He probably thought this was high enough for safety."

"But it wasn't," Judy finished tragically. Then her eyes dilated with horror. "There he is! Right behind that tree! Oh! He must be dead."

"He's moving!" cried Peter. "Maybe we can still save him."

Judy was the first to reach the prostrate form on the ground.

"Horace! Horace! Speak to me," she cried, bending over him and clasping both of his hands in hers. "Are you badly hurt?"

He turned over and blinked up at her. "Only a little, here on my head—and awfully dizzy. I guess I fell out of the tree. Or maybe I jumped," he mumbled. "I sort of remember climbing up there and seeing that dam grinning at me . . . wider . . . wider. . . ."

"Your clothes are damp!" she exclaimed. "Maybe you were knocked out when the flood came."

"The flood?" he questioned dazedly. "What flood?"

Judy glanced helplessly at her companions. "Is he delirious?" She felt of his head. "Oh, I wish Dad were here," she cried. "He needs a doctor and—we both need our father."

Suddenly Horace sat up and faced them. "What is that policeman doing here?" he demanded and then broke off in a frenzied cry, "I won't go with him. I—I won't do it again. I'm not crazy anymore."

"Nobody thinks you're crazy," Judy reassured him quietly. "We just want to take you home."

"Home?" he questioned in a more rational tone of voice. "Is it still there?"

"Well, to Grandma's," she amended.

"And then what are you going to do with me, Judy?"

"Do with you!" exclaimed the policeman. "Plenty, I guess. There's a couple of thousand people waiting to get a glimpse of you. They'll probably want you to make a speech."

"Gee! They *do* want to make a fool of me.

As if I hadn't been fool enough already!"

"You haven't been a fool, Horace. You've been a hero." It was Judy's reassuring voice that told him this.

"Tell me what's happened," he pleaded. "I'm not really hurt, you see. It was just that —that I had an awful feeling. I thought I was going nuts."

"It's the crowd on the hillside who are going nuts," Peter put in. "They think you were killed. They won't go away until you are found. Come, can you walk?"

"Let me see. I want to get my bearings first." Horace stood up unsteadily and looked out across the valley. He stared for a moment at the pitiful wreck of the town that had been Roulsville. Then he screamed and threw himself, face down, on the ground.

"It can't be true! It can't be true!" he moaned. "This must be madness! That grinning dam has set me crazy and I'm seeing things—seeing things—" His voice trailed off in an incoherent mumble.

CHAPTER XXI

THE DEAD MAN'S STORY

"I'LL go for the car," Arthur volunteered, "and park it in the road right below. We've got to get Dr. Bolton across the valley someway. Horace's head may be seriously hurt."

"Oh, Arthur," cried Judy, "and it's my fault for making him ride the colt."

"If he hadn't been on the colt I'd like to know how he could have warned the people. Like as not you would all be dead," the officer said gravely.

"I warned the people?" Horace had been listening. "Why, I thought I dreamed that. I—I heard such a crash and I thought I was in bed having another of those horrible nightmares and it was Judy rapping on the wall. 'Member, Sis, like you did the other night?"

"I—I remember," she cried. "Imagine how I felt, Horace. So proud that you were a hero —and then to think that you might be dead."

"Proud?" he asked, getting to his feet excitedly. "Really proud——"

But Judy threw her arms around him and smothered the rest of his sentence with a kiss.

"You bet she's proud," exclaimed the policeman. "And who wouldn't be? Boy! You couldn't save the houses, but you saved the people—just about all of them."

"Then there was somebody killed?" he cried in alarm.

"Just one, a Mr. Rubin, the boss at the paper mill. They found his body. There are still some people who can't get across the valley. We couldn't make a check-up of the missing," the policeman added. "So far, you were the only one."

"Are your family all safe?" he asked Peter.

"All of them," the boy replied. "Even the cat had sense enough to follow."

"And Grandfather?"

"Sam Tucker's house wasn't flooded," Judy reassured him.

"What about Dad and Mother?" he asked anxiously. "I didn't see them. Did they come home?"

"Just before the flood, but they're safe on the other side of the valley. I guess Dad's looking after someone that was hurt." Judy was careful not to tell him that she was still uncertain about her mother. That white sheeted person—but it was big enough to be a man and Mrs. Bolton lacked an inch of being as tall as her daughter.

"There's a crew of men and boys clearing away the wreckage," the police officer put in. "Your folks will come across as soon as they can. Here, boy, you need assistance. Take a hold of my arm."

It was true. Horace did need assistance. It took quite an effort for him to move his legs. They had been cramped from his long stay in the same position on the damp ground after all that bumping on the colt's back.

Arthur returned presently and quite a crowd of boys were with him. Among them, Donald Carter. After more excited explanations they all started back to the pavilion where most of the survivors of the disaster waited.

"I managed to get through with my car," Arthur said. "It's waiting down there in the road. Probably it won't hold all of you but Horace, at least, can ride."

A better view of the town was afforded from the road and the results of the flood were plainly to be seen as the car made its way back to the park. Not a house was left intact with the exception of those on Hill Street. Trees, parts of buildings and débris of all kinds made the road impassable except on the upper side.

Horace did not feel inclined to talk of his experiences just yet. He had to figure out something plausible to say before he dared trust his own tongue. To their many questions he replied, "I'll tell you about it later after I've had a chance to think."

When the crowd on the hillside caught sight of Arthur's car with Horace sitting comfortably beside the driver, they arose as one and gave a mighty cheer. It could be heard clear across the valley where those who had taken refuge in the houses along Hill Street waved and shouted and even climbed on roofs in order to make sure that Horace was actually alive and safe. In the park the people were shouting themselves hoarse. Ginger, the colt which had arrived ahead of its master, was tied just outside the pavilion.

At the insistence of the crowd, Horace was borne on the shoulders of Peter and Arthur and placed on Ginger's back where he smiled a greeting to the two thousand people who owed their lives to him.

After that he was bundled up in a blanket and

served with hot coffee and doughnuts while
people stood around singing and cheering.
Judy's eyes were fixed on him as if he were a
phantom brother who might suddenly disappear. In rare moments she had imagined him
as a successful reporter, but never as a hero.
Photographers were busy taking his picture,
in the car, on the colt, eating doughnuts. It
did not matter where, just so they got a snap
of him. Horace, hearing the click of moving
picture cameras, felt conscious of every motion.
Fortunately, the pictures would not be in color
or they would have shown a blush which had
once earned him the nickname of "Salmon
Face." "Salmon Face Sister" they had called
him. But now the same boys were cheering
and calling him the hero of Roulsville. It
struck him as being a bit funny and he forgot
his self-consciousness and began to laugh while
cameras clicked faster than ever.

In the midst of all this, who should arrive
on the scene but Dr. Bolton himself. His had
been the first car to cross the valley and it was
completely spattered with mud. Judy was relieved and overjoyed to see her mother beside
him but in the rear, stretched across the seat
cushions, was the motionless form of a man.

"Sorry we couldn't come sooner, son."

Mrs. Bolton clasped Horace in her arms and the doctor patted his shoulder.

"That's all right, Dad," he replied. "I can see you've been busy at your usual job of trying to save lives."

"You're the one who saved lives, my boy," his father told him. "Come, Mother and I want to hear how it happened. We don't seem to have the story straight in our minds."

"I did nothing brave," Horace began.

Arthur, hearing their voices, rushed up to Dr. Bolton and hastened to explain. "Nothing brave! Why, we have Horace to thank for everything. He sounded the warning forty minutes before the flood came. How he knew it, nobody knows. I told him once that nothing short of a miracle could save the people in Roulsville if that dam broke. Well, Dr. Bolton, your son performed the miracle."

The doctor shook his head. "I didn't think you had it in you, Horace. Forgive your old Dad, won't you?"

His mother's eyes were bright with tears. No one could accuse her of spoiling her son now that he was a hero.

The people still stood watching. Someone

suggested a parade and a cry of approval went up from the crowd. Dr. Bolton's car was made ready. They removed the dead man from the rear seat. They pushed him on to a stretcher and signalled for an ambulance to take him.

"Poor fellow," murmured the doctor. "I was with him till the last. He was trying to tell me something. It seems he had been hiding in the paper mill and didn't hear the alarm. He kept screaming that he was a murderer and I couldn't seem to make him understand that the people had all been saved."

"He may have gone crazy," Arthur suggested.

"Perhaps," Dr. Bolton agreed. "His head was horribly crushed. But, somehow, I think he knew what he was talking about. He may have had something to do with the construction of the dam."

Judy had been gazing at the frightful countenance of the dead man. His head was swathed in bandages from his eyes upward, giving him the gruesome aspect of a mummy. His mouth was set in a hard line and the pallor of his swarthy skin was emphasized by his stubbly black beard.

"Oh! And it was my fault," she cried out

suddenly. "I just as good as killed that man."

"Child! Child!" her father reproved. "What could you have done to save him?"

Between hysterical sobs, she related the story of Dry Brook. How she, thinking someone had changed its course for the sake of revenge, had deliberately dug the barrier away.

"The dam wouldn't have broken if it hadn't been for me. That man would still be alive and we would still have our home." Judy's shoulders were shaking with sobs.

"Come! Come!" The doctor chided gently. "You don't think a dam the size of that one up in the woods would be strong enough to check Dry Brook in such a storm as we had. Why! That little embankment would have been washed away in five minutes."

"You really think so?"

"I know it," declared the doctor and Horace added, "That note you wrote really did more good than checking Dry Brook could have possibly done. You dared me to ride the colt and that note seemed like a dare too when I read it. I simply had to do something to prove to you that I wasn't a coward. Don't you see, Judy, if it hadn't been for you I couldn't have been a hero and the people in Roulsville would

not have been saved. I would have always been
a sissy and now, whatever I have been, I feel
sure that I shall never be afraid of little things
again.''

"Don't, Horace," pleaded Judy, "please,
please, don't praise me when I'm so sorry and
ashamed.''

"Didn't they praise me when I felt the same
way?" he charged. "We did foolish things,
both of us, but both of us had high motives in
doing them. Do you think I don't know it was
because you cared about me, Judy, that you
pestered me and teased me and tried to make a
man of me? Of course I know. And you have
succeeded, too, I hope. Whatever other people
may say, *I know* that the heroine of the Roulsville flood is you.''

"No! No! Horace, don't say that. I might
have killed you with my wicked dare.''

"And I might have been called a lunatic instead of a hero—if the dam hadn't broken.
You see, it is what happened that counts, not
what might have happened.''

Her mother pressed Judy's hand and said
tenderly, "Believe him, dear, and don't blame
yourself any more.''

But Horace was not left alone with his family

for long. Reporters from his own and other papers pressed around, eager to hear his story.

"How did you find out that the dam was going to break?" Donald Carter insisted. "Everybody will be wanting to know that."

"Tell them it was all a blooming accident," replied Horace wearily. "Then maybe I'll talk about it later."

"That's right," agreed Judy, elbowing her way through the crowd and taking her brother's arm.

Lois had slipped up beside her to tell her that Mrs. Dobbs was tired and ready to start for home.

"She's waiting in your car but if you don't have room for her she can come up in ours. Arthur promised to be back again in the morning so that you can see the papers. I suppose Horace's photograph will be on every front page."

"Really!"

"Why, of course," explained Lois. "He's an honest-to-goodness hero. Aren't you proud of him?"

Judy nodded. "Very proud, even if I don't quite understand this premonition business."

"And I am proud of my brother too," put in

Lois, as, arm in arm, the two girls walked toward the doctor's car. "I can't help believing that his anxiety about the dam had something to do with the people being saved."

"It surely did," spoke up Horace. "Arthur and Judy deserve all the credit, really. I'm due to talk to some more reporters this evening and I'll tell them a few things they wouldn't listen to this afternoon. Judy, do you suppose Grandma's got anything to eat in the house? How many of this crowd will we dare bring home?"

"I wish we could bring them all. We'll need some people to help us celebrate."

"Your brother won't want much more celebrating, my dear," spoke up Mrs. Dobbs quietly, "but we'll try and not be noisy and anywhere to sleep will do. You see, we haven't any home now, but we can be thankful we have each other. Did you notice the cat, honey? Here she is, sleeping under my shawl."

"Blackberry's mother!" exclaimed Judy. "And I doubt if she misses her kitten as much as I do. It's wonderful to be all safe and on our way to Grandma's," she reflected, "but I'm afraid that I shall never be contented until this shadow man they call Christopher White is caught and I have Blackberry back again."

After the car was on its way, heading a long parade, Peter glanced at Judy and then at the little hut beside the road.

"There's nothing on the roof now," he observed. "Maybe those policemen you sent back there did catch him."

CHAPTER XXII

WHEN they arrived at the Smeed farm quite a crowd rushed forward to congratulate Horace. The minister of River Street church always thoughtful of others, had remembered Mrs. Smeed and had been the first one to tell her the good news. Grandfather Smeed and Sam Tucker as well as some of his parishioners had accompanied him.

An aroma of hot apple pies greeted Horace as he burst into the kitchen and gathered his grandmother in his arms.

"Hot pies! Of all things! Grandma! If you aren't a wonder!"

"Well," she explained, "I just had to do something. It wouldn't do to let my nerves get the best of me again. So I baked a batch of pies and prayed God there'd be somebody spared to eat them. Then the good pastor rapped at the door and when I saw who it was I fainted again and let a pie burn black around the edges. He brought me to and told me

everything. My baby boy! I should have
known you'd do something splendid."

All during supper Horace evaded questions
and remained silent except when spoken to.

Much to their surprise, telegrams of con-
gratulation began coming in before they were
finished with their late meal. Not only congratulations but offers of all kinds.

Judy read the telegrams aloud to her brother
and could not understand his calm manner
when the rest of them were so excited.

"Here's one from the governor," she cried,
waving a yellow slip excitedly. "He says the
people of this state owe you a debt of gratitude
that they can never repay."

"Then I wish they wouldn't try," answered
Horace shortly as he tossed the telegram aside.
"Just look at all these crazy offers and in the
morning's mail I suppose there'll be even more.
Wouldn't I be a ninny to accept checks and
positions from people I don't even know? Remember when I took your share of our money,
Judy? Well, you won't catch me doing anything like that again."

"But this is so different," argued Judy as
she opened another telegram and handed it to
her brother. He was shocked and amused to

find that he had been invited to join a musical show.

"Imagine me in a song and dance act," he chuckled. "Fly-little-birdie-fly stuff or maybe I should ride a white horse across the stage. Lend me your scarf, Judy, and away I shall flutter."

In spite of his jocular manner, Horace was, in reality, deeply worried. All his life he had received the best that his parents had to give. Now the whole country was offering the best that they had, and Horace felt that he did not deserve it.

"Judy," he said, "you've been pining for something to do. How would you like to act as my secretary and return all this junk, saying that your brother is not interested in accepting favors or receiving gifts?"

"Return everything, Horace?"

"Yes, everything but the congratulations and I won't be getting them much longer."

Judy saw what he meant later that evening when Donald Carter and six other reporters came. Mrs. Smeed escorted them to the living room and treated them in her most hospitable fashion. She and his mother both seemed glad of all the praise that their boy was receiving, believing, as they all did, that he justly deserved it.

Horace, still a bit unsteady on his legs, entered the room and seated himself in the midst of the group of reporters.

"Well, are you ready to talk?" they asked good-naturedly.

"Yes, I am," he replied, motioning the rest of them into the living room. "And all of you must come in and listen for I have a confession to make—and I want everybody to hear it."

The reporters listened to Horace's story eagerly. His grandparents kept near him, anxious to hear while Dr. Bolton leaned forward in his chair and drank in every word. Mr. and Mrs. Dobbs watched the boy almost as intently as did his mother and Judy and Peter were perfectly quiet.

He told the story of his great fear from beginning to end and blamed himself for acting like a coward and a fool.

"You see," he finished. "It was, as I said before, just an accident. When I heard that first clap of thunder I went crazy with fear. I couldn't think. It all seems so absurd now, my racing through town that way. It's a wonder anybody listened to me. I wish you could get the idea out of people's heads that I am a hero. Nobody but myself would have been fool enough to do what I did That'll be a funny story to put in the papers after what must have already gone to press, but I'm doing my duty and telling the whole truth. I'm nothing but a coward and a sissy, always was and always will be. Tell them that!

"I went out of church feeling like a new man. The minister had preached a fine sermon on Courage and I had determined to live up to it. I was scared to death of the colt and only rode him because my sister dared me to. She had set me to thinking and if anyone deserves credit for what I did it is Judy. She is the heroine of the flood and if you don't believe it, I'll read you the letter she wrote. And," he added as he drew forth the note from his pocket, "if it hadn't been for her courage I would never have been fired with the mad ambition to make her proud of me. I say "Mad ambition" because I still believe I was half crazy when I heard that thunder. You see, it was only thunder and I thought it was the dam. Well, I forgot my determination to be courageous——"

Here one of the reporters stopped him. "How do you figure that, young man?" he asked. "Wasn't it your determination to be courageous that sent you racing *toward* the stricken town instead of away from it?"

"No." Horace's voice carried conviction. "The colt whirled around all by himself. I had nothing to do with that."

"But you didn't try to turn him back. You didn't try to stop him, did you? You didn't take to the hills yourself until the streets of Roulsville were empty. Don't you call that courage?"

"Of course it's courage," spoke up Peter Dobbs. "Especially when he believed the flood was almost upon him."

"It's the kind of courage all of us need," added Donald. "Your actions speak for themselves, Sister. We don't need such lengthy explanations and apologies."

Sister! The old nickname. But there was a ring to Donald's voice and even if the nickname clung folks would know it was irony, like the fat boy who is usually called "Skinny."

"But you can, at least, see why I cannot accept favors," Horace argued. "If I really had been a hero it would have been bad enough. I want you all to understand that I will accept nothing. Put that in the papers too."

"It's like a hero to refuse such favors," remarked one of the reporters with a smile.

"I'm afraid you don't understand even yet." Horace was still trying to convince the reporters, but they would not be convinced.

"Indeed we do understand. You couldn't have told your story more clearly. We understand everything but you're the hero of the Roulsville flood just the same. Your friend, Pett, will come in for his share and also your sister."

"Wait till you hear her story," Horace cried. "It will make mine look sick. Do you realize that Judy was kidnaped by this strange person, Christopher White, who seems to be able to appear and disappear whenever he feels like it? She was imprisoned all night in a lonely hut and tortured until she promised not to tell what she knew of the dam. But the clever girl only promised not to speak. Perhaps you have noticed how unusually quiet she is." He smiled understandingly at Judy. "Well, she wrote it all out—the conversation that proved the engineer, the workmen and some officials of the paper company knew that the dam might break with the next hard storm. Charlie Austin was connected with it too——"

"Why, the police are holding him for questioning," Donald Carter exclaimed. "Somebody telephoned just when the dam broke. The
conversation was cut in two. That mysterious
call will be on the front page of the morning
paper."

"You might add that I was the one who made
it," Judy spoke up quietly.

CHAPTER XXIII

UNMASKING THE SHADOW

THE next day Lois and Arthur came in their car with a high stack of city papers. Everybody, including the Dobbs family, grouped around and searched through them eagerly. On every front page was Horace's picture and on some Horace and Judy together. Underneath these latter it said, "HORACE BOLTON, HERO OF THE ROULSVILLE FLOOD AND HIS SISTER JUDY WHO PREDICTED THE DISASTER."

Three papers printed Horace's story just as he had told it to the reporters but headlines ran, "MODEST HERO REFUSES TO ACCEPT PRAISE FOR COURAGE" or "COURAGEOUS BOY HERO CALLS HIMSELF 'SISSY.' "

Pictures of the devastated Roulsville accompanied those of Horace and Judy. Even Ginger had not been overlooked. The Farringdon *Daily Herald* devoted its whole pictorial section to these scenes. Arthur's picture was among them and a paragraph told of his efforts to prevent the flood.

Some papers of the previous day were in the stack. These spoke of the hero as missing and so, Lois said, many thousands would be anxiously awaiting the news of his whereabouts. Judy tried to imagine other girls, like herself, who might be reading and thinking of Horace that very minute.

"And don't forget there are other boys who might be reading the papers and thinking of you," Arthur gibed good-naturedly.

"There sure are," Peter agreed from his chair by the window.

Judy had been so absorbed in the description of the flood and her own and her brother's part in it that she almost overlooked the heading, "ENGINEER MISSING" on the opposite side of the paper.

Authorities, it said, were trying to fix the blame. The Rite-Way Construction Company, builders of the dam, had gone out of business. Its offices were abandoned. They were holding Charlie Austin for questioning and were still hunting for Christopher White, the missing engineer.

"It says they searched the hut and found nothing but his cloak," Judy continued, reading the paper aloud. "Honestly," she confessed, "it does sound spooky—and interesting—now that we're all safe and can breathe freely. I shall be on pins and needles until we hear more about this mystery."

"Which will not be very long," Peter Dobbs prophesied. He was peering out toward the road and Judy rushed to the window to see what had drawn his attention.

"Charlie Austin!" she exclaimed. "And those two policemen are bringing him here!"

Immediately the whole house was a-quiver with excitement. Dr. Bolton, outwardly calm, escorted them to the living room and Judy recognized at once the officers who had searched the hut.

"We can't get anything out of this fellow," the taller one said gruffly, "and since you're the one who called up perhaps you can help us. Have you any genuine proof that he knows something about the dam?"

"I know he bribed a friend of mine to keep still about it," Judy replied fearlessly. "And a workman who was killed in the flood tried to bribe me."

"Tried to!" Charlie Austin sniffed. "You mean, did, but you turned out to be a rotten squealer."

Judy stared at him. There was something sinister about the distortions of his face.

"You'll have to handcuff him, officer, if you want me to question him," she directed. "He looks as if he might spring at me."

"He is quick," the policeman agreed, and even as he said it Charlie bolted for the door. Peter and Arthur together headed him off but there was quite a struggle before he was handcuffed and jerked to position again.

He stood facing Judy, his eyes burning with hatred.

"I'd like to know how you found out I ever made any promises," she charged. "And if you can prove that I broke my pledged word, I'd just like to see you do it."

"You promised not to speak——"

"She didn't speak," Horace broke in, "she wrote a letter."

The policeman chuckled.

"You must have been there yourself to know so much about it, Charlie Austin," Judy went on. "Where were you hiding?"

"I wasn't there," he replied.

Judy realized that she had heard that high-pitched voice before. She walked around behind him and scrutinized his handcuffed hands. They were long and thin and chalk-white except where he had polished his nails with pink polish. Then she noticed that the part in his hair went at an angle—and it had not done so before the scuffle.

"Officer," she said with a provoking smile. "I guess you'd give a lot to be able to turn Christopher White over to the authorities."

"You bet I would," he cried, forgetting his dignity in a burst of boyish enthusiasm.

Judy was quivering with excitement while the others stood around the room in groups, tense and expectant.

"Suppose you remove Charlie Austin's hair."

"His hair!" exclaimed the officer, tightening his hold on the prisoner as he tried to wrench away.

"Remove his hair," Judy repeated. "That black wig he's got on. You might erase his penciled eyebrows too while you're at it and rub a little of the rouge off his face."

"Judy!" gasped Horace. "What are you saying?"

The policeman, however, understood perfectly and did as she told him.

Before the horrified gaze of the ten people who were watching stood a man who looked like a ghost. His hairless head resembled a skull. All that he needed was a long black cloak and the illusion would have been complete.

CHAPTER XXIV

THE policemen were ready to leave. They had their man.

"And if I know anything about our state prisons the Vanishing Shadow won't do any more vanishing for quite a spell."

"Unless he crawls out through the roof," Judy put in, half in earnest.

"Say!" exclaimed the tall officer. "What are you trying to do, kid me?"

"No. Why?"

"Because I don't intend scrambling over very many more roofs to rescue stranded cats."

"What do you mean?" Judy asked in genuine bewilderment.

"All I can tell you is that when we searched the roof of that hut the way you suggested we found a little black kitten——"

"Oh!" exclaimed Judy. "Did it have a white nose and white feet?"

"It sure did," the officer replied, grinning.

Judy turned to Charlie Austin, alias Chris-

topher White, "And you didn't know what happened to my kitten," she derided him.

"Did he steal it?" the officer demanded.

"Yes, he did," Judy replied. "He seems
to have had an idea that he could scare me.
But after looking at his face I doubt if I shall
ever be afraid of anything."

"And we'll see that you get your kitten
back," the policeman promised.

"There will be a trial," Dr. Bolton said after
the policemen had left with their strange prisoner, "and no doubt, you will all be called upon
to testify. You must remember, Judy, that you
are sworn to tell the whole truth."

"I know, Dad, but do I need to tell them
about Dry Brook and that little dam?"

"That's the very thing I mean," he answered. "Tell them, just as you told me, that
you thought Charlie Austin was plotting some
kind of revenge. Don't you see, Judy, that
your testimony will be important?"

"Because if they know he changed Dry
Brook's course, they will know he realized the
dam wasn't safe and kept quiet about it. Is
that it, Dad?"

"Yes, Judy. And," he went on, "you must
tell them about the bribes. Don't even try to

spare Edna. The chances are she won't get a sentence. The only others involved, I believe, are those workmen who are all dead. Remember, dear girl, there are no secrets and no mysteries at a trial."

"I'll remember, Dad," Judy promised. "The next time a mystery comes up I won't try to solve it all by myself."

"No!" cried a chorus of voices. "We'll help you." Arthur, Lois, Peter and Horace did not intend to be left out.

The Dobbs family were moving to Farringdon. They left two days later but not before Blackberry had been restored to his mistress. Old Checker was reunited with her kitten only to be separated again. Horace also went back to his newspaper job where he would receive more praise and adulation.

"Just what he needs to keep up his spirits," Dr. Bolton declared.

"You look as if you need something to keep up your own spirits," his daughter observed as she sat watching him.

"Yes," he said. "It's going to be a hard pull. It isn't easy to establish practice in a strange town and there's little hope of Roulsville being rebuilt. I'll need your help, Judy girl."

There was a new home to be considered and
all new equipment for his office. That would
take money but Judy knew her father would
never allow her to quit school and work. That
wasn't the kind of help he meant.

She turned over the paper that she held in
her hand. Twice she started to speak and then
changed her mind. Horace had instructed her
to return all gifts, no matter what, and here
someone had offered them a house in Farringdon, rent free.

It was Sunday, a week later. Bluebird, wings
folded and purring motor silenced, rested in
front of the Smeed home after her flying trip
to Dry Brook Hollow. Horace, still the center
of attraction, sat in the midst of an interested
group on the front porch. Nobody noticed that
Lois and Judy had quietly slipped away.

"I'm so glad you could come," exclaimed
Judy as soon as they were alone. "I have a
big surprise for you. Listen, Lois. Horace
has said he wouldn't accept any favors. Well,
we've *got* to make him accept this one. I'm
counting on you as my best friend to help me
out of an awful mix up."

"Are you being mysterious on purpose?"
asked Lois, looking bewildered.

"No, but if Horace is mad——"

"I thought Horace never got mad."

"He didn't used to. But since the flood he's changed so that you never can tell what he will do. He has reason to be mad this time."

"Judy, what *are* you talking about?"

"About the house in Farringdon where we are going to live.

"Horace asked me to open his mail and send back all checks and gifts. I did it, much as I hated to, until a letter came from a Mr. Vincent in Farringdon. He offered us a house, rent free, and it's on Grove Street. I couldn't refuse that when Dad was worrying so, I just came down here and thought things out. Really, it seems best for all of us and still I feel afraid. Lois, I wrote and told him we'd take the house."

"A house on Grove Street?" questioned Lois. "Judy, was it number thirteen hundred and sixty-five?"

"Yes, yes, how did you know?"

"I can be mysterious too," laughed Lois. "Now we'll go back and face the enemy. Judy, will you let me do the talking?"

"Gladly," she replied, much relieved.

When they entered the house a hot supper was waiting. Horace and his father were sitting at the table busily engaged in a conversation. Dr. Bolton was trying to decide where they should move. His patients were scattered now but most of them had gone to manufacturing towns in the southern part of the state.

"That would take you a long way from us," Mrs. Smeed said. "Horace and Judy will miss their grandparents."

Here Lois broke in on the conversation.

"Perhaps I could suggest a way out."

"No, Lois," said her brother. "This is a family affair. You had better keep quiet."

"Did you ever know me to keep quiet," she retorted, "when I had something important to say? Dr. Bolton, how would you like to live in Farringdon?"

"Well," he began. "I've lived in Roulsville all my life but Farringdon seems almost as much like home. We have friends there and it would not be hard to establish a practice. But real estate is sky high——"

"Suppose you got a house rent free," interrupted Lois.

"What *are* you talking about?" demanded Arthur. "This is no time for fairy tales. Dr. Bolton's up against a serious proposition."

"And," Lois pointed out, "Judy and I have

a serious answer for it. Arthur, did you ever hear anything unusual about number thirteen hundred and sixty-five Grove Street?"

"Did I?" he exclaimed. "I should say so!"

Lois laughed. "I thought so. Now listen, everybody, while I tell you something simply thrilling. Harry Vincent, an old miser with loads of money, couldn't rent number thirteen hundred and sixty-five because a rumor has spread around town that the house is haunted. So he very generously offered it to Horace, thinking, I presume, that ghosts wouldn't bother a hero. Unfortunately, he had instructed Judy to open his mail. She accepted the offer in a letter she wrote last week."

"You did!" cried Horace, glaring at Judy. "How dared you answer my letter?"

"You told her to open it," chided Lois gently.

"But not to answer it, I say——"

"Here! Here!" reproved Dr. Bolton. "Horace, I thought you two were never going to quarrel again. It looks to me as though Judy has used good judgment. And as for the house being haunted, that, we know, is nonsense."

"Probably it's nothing but creaky stairs," put in Mrs. Bolton.

"Oh dear," sighed Judy. "I suppose it is. But as soon as Lois said it, I felt all quivery. Really, there must be something spooky about the place or people wouldn't be afraid to live in it. We can find out the reason for the rumor at least and maybe have a ghost party to make things more exciting."

"Now don't get to planning things just yet," objected Dr. Bolton. "It's up to Horace. Do we take the house or don't we?"

"Aw, go ahead and take it," replied Horace, "ghosts and all. It's no loss to this Harry Vincent if nobody else will live in it and I must confess the ghost idea is interesting."

"Horace, you are an angel!" cried Judy, throwing her arms around her brother's neck and kissing him.

Around and around the room she danced, clapping her hands in ecstasies of delight and hugging first one and then another. Horace backed into a corner to ward off a second attack. Nothing daunted, Judy took it out on Lois.

"How perfectly marvelous!" she sang out. "Lois, imagine it! We will go to high school together and I'll get acquainted with all your friends. You have such a lot of them. Why,

I'll be making a new friend every day!''

"My! My!" laughed Arthur. "You're expecting a lot of Farringdon."

"She deserves a lot," Horace put in. "She was right about the house, too. If the so-called hero of the flood would not accept such an extraordinary offer then the heroine surely had a right to do so."

"So say we all," came Arthur's answer from the car. "Hop in, Lois. What about you, Horace? I supose you'll be wanting to stay and help your folks pack up."

"I wish I could," he replied, "but I'll be needed to help get the paper out. Goodbye, all. See you in Farringdon."

Judy's gray eyes followed the car as it rolled away. Then she turned and caught up the little black kitten and laughed to think how he had frightened her. After all it had been exciting— solving the mystery of the shadow. And this was only the beginning. More and more adventures were in store for the girl.

Lois, Arthur and Horace were calling goodbyes from the car. Judy waved her hand, and Blackberry waved the plume that was his tail.

THE END

CPSIA information can be obtained
at www.ICGtesting.com
Printed in the USA
LVHW091620280819
629259LV00002B/272/P